The Girl Who Sang with the Beatles
and Other Stories

The Girl Who Sang with the Beatles

And Other Stories by

Robert Hemenway

For
Elizabeth

Contents

The Girl Who Sang with the Beatles
and Other Stories

Stories

My father came home one evening in early spring about two months before my sister was born to find my mother standing, hand to head, on the oval rag rug in the living room, wearing the brown wool bathrobe she had put on when she got up twelve hours before. She had not even combed her hair. I was in my bedroom reading when he rang the downstairs bell, and when Mother did not answer and he rang again I buzzed him in. I told him she didn't feel well, though that was plain. I had come home from school at three thirty to find her in the same condition, sitting on a chair in the dining alcove with the apartment door wide open.

She stood in the center of the rug in the living room and called out to my father, who was taking off his rubbers and his overcoat in the front hall ten feet away. "Come and look, John!" she said. "You can stand right here on this spot and see everything we own." She had been going through the apartment since before five o'clock, opening and shutting drawers and doors, turning on every light in the place though it wasn't yet dark. My father stood behind her and put both hands on her shoulders, but she pulled away and began to cry. "It's all so ugly," she said. I was sent down to the drugstore for ice cream, and when I got back my mother was lying under the quilt in their bedroom and my father was cooking up some ham and eggs.

My mother liked pretty things, and there were few in that Chicago apartment except those she brought from home or made herself. We had moved to Chicago four years before from Meredith, the Michigan town across the lake where my father and mother were brought up, where they were married, and where I was born. My father had been in the insurance business there with his brother, but he wanted to get away from home and break Mother away from her family, and he took a job in Chicago with Cudahy Packing, in the accounting office. Though he made more each week than he had in Meredith, it couldn't have gone much beyond our food and rent, and there was no longer any family around to ease the strain. My mother had to work, too. She taught kindergarten in the same school that I went to—I was eight then and already in the fourth grade—but she had to quit after the first term, with the baby expected in May.

So long as Mother was working, she was all right. (These are my father's words; I've heard them a hundred times.) Once she stopped teaching, she began to worry. She tried to keep busy. She painted the bedroom suite robin's-egg blue—it took three coats to cover the mahogany stain—and decorated the bureau drawers and the bedstead with hand-painted roses. She made gesso picture frames, modelled figures out of clay she had brought home from the school storeroom, and painted glass bottles and vases. Once she made bread. I came home from school that day to find her on her knees on the living-room floor, the rug pushed aside, pressing and pounding dough on a piece of floured yellow oilcloth. The loaves rose unevenly and burned, and she wept. Tears came easily for her, and rages.

She must have hated the apartment. I could not; it was home. The place was always dark—only the two windows in the living room opened on a street—and we lived there like a family of bears. Or like displaced persons. My mother and father had few friends and little money for pleasure. What there was they spent on trips back home to Meredith, which could only have kept alive my mother's nostalgia and discontent.

My mother's family, the Bishops, were very close. Her father, a doctor, had prospered in Meredith and built a large, comfortable house with rooms for each of the children—three daughters and a son—that were kept for them after they moved away. None of the children stayed away for long. Mother and I spent our summers there even after we moved to Chicago.

I slept lightly the night of my mother's nervous breakdown— that was what my father finally came to call it, though it seems to me now that she was like a woman bereaved, as if she knew what was to come—and I woke now and then to hear her low, persistent voice and my father's, dry and rough sometimes, and then with a high twang as if he were a child complaining. Later I woke and the apartment was quiet, though the lights were still on. I went out into the living room and saw them sitting at the table in the dining alcove. My father was drinking coffee, my mother looking into her cup. I remember feeling something secret and frightening between them—as if I had come upon them in an embrace. They did not see me. I was afraid one of them would punish me, and I went back to bed.

My mother and I went to Meredith the next Saturday to stay at the Bishop place until the baby was born. She couldn't stand it any longer in Chicago, she told Father that night and me the next day. She had to go home, back to her own house and her own room, where there were people to take care of her. She was worn out. And she was sick and tired of having to do all the housework, scrubbing floors down on her knees. She wanted to have her baby in Meredith. Her father had been in the delivery room when I was born. (Years later, I learned that he had delivered me.) She wouldn't feel safe with anyone but him.

Father drove us over and drove back to Chicago on Sunday, back to work. He must have been angry and hurt at first, and not only because he would be living alone. He had left Meredith to get Mother away from the Bishops; now, at the first crisis, she was going straight back again and he would be still further in their debt. He wanted to be completely on his own. He considered himself an independent man. Yet on that night, I imagine, when my mother let out all at once the things she wanted and hated and feared, my father resisted her at first and then gave in, with his stomach knotting at the thought of our leaving him. And then, once he had let himself be swayed and once he had telephoned Meredith and wakened the doctor and Mrs. Bishop to tell them Mother and I would be coming, he must have been relieved and ready for us to go. For a time, the responsibility would not be his. He could do his work in peace, knowing that Mother and I were safe.

As for me, I was glad to be leaving Chicago. For one thing, it meant no more school that year. School bored me; I'd been reading since I was four and little was said in a classroom that I didn't know. There would be no need for me to go to classes in Meredith, my mother said; she would teach me. Good. And I loved the Bishop house. It was huge. Aunts and uncles and cousins lived nearby; I was the only small boy in the family just then, and a favorite. They spoiled me, and I luxuriated there. Snapshots taken in Meredith at the time all show me smiling the same silly, helpless smile.

We were out of the apartment and on our way by seven that Saturday morning; from Chicago to Meredith, thirty-five years ago, was an all-day drive. The three of us sat in front, with me by the window. The back of the car was piled high with bags and parcels and my toys. I waved goodbye to things along the road. I thought I was clever; it was a baby trick that I knew annoyed my father. "Goodbye, house!" I cried, waving out the window. "Goodbye, school! Goodbye, streetcar!" Through Jackson Park, through Hammond (Goodbye, gas tanks), through Gary, through Michigan City (in Indiana!), and up into Michigan on Highway 31, past sand dunes held together by scrub oak and maple and beach grass and studded with jack pine. I read signs out loud. "EATS." "Time to Retire." "Pop's on Ice and Ma's Inside." "Jesus Saves."

"What, Bobby?" my father would say to me sometimes in spite of himself.

"Nothing. I'm reading," I would say. I got on his nerves. He was whistling bugle calls, softly, from in back of his teeth. "You gotta get up, you gotta get up in the morning!" "Soupie, soupie, soupie, not a single bean!" He had been an Army captain in the war.

We drove straight to the Bishop house and up the driveway into the back yard. The sun was already low, and the bedroom and attic windows on the west side of the house blazed orange. My grandmother, a tiny, nervous woman, stood on the concrete front steps waiting for us. She waved once, and by the time we had gone around the corner and turned into the back yard she was already there. My grandfather and my mother's younger sister, Aunt Elda, were just behind her. Mother and I were embraced, caught up, and swept into the house like the queen and her crown prince come home. My father and the Doctor waited and came on behind.

Dr. Bishop had built his house in 1903, soon after he had moved to Meredith from Corinth, a village nearby, and while his children were young. The house, a three-story gabled building of brick and stucco, sat on a double corner lot, surrounded by grass, trees, and flowers, at the corner of Utica and Superior Streets, a few blocks from the center of town. There was grass everywhere, to the west a lawn broad enough for games of softball and croquet, to the east a shady yard where only feathery grass and lilies of the valley would grow. There were good climbing trees—a black cherry that bore fruit pillaged by the robins and sparrows before it grew ripe, and a silver maple, and a Japanese walnut whose nutmeats were shaped like wrinkled hearts. The garage had a rose trellis in front that could be climbed and a roof low enough in back to jump from. After a few minutes in the living room, I excused myself and went outside. We hadn't been there since Christmas, and I wanted to see how things were now that it was spring. Crocuses, yellow and purple, were in bloom on the west lawn, still winter brown but mottled with pale green; daffodil shoots were breaking out of the soil along the side of the house. My grandfather's tan coupé was parked in front, and I got in and sat behind the wheel. The car smelled of wintergreen and iodoform. I felt myself master of the house, and my father a visitor, come just for the day. And for a few weeks after that life seemed to give me whatever I asked of it. My mother and I had never been so close. Except for Sundays, when my father came, I had her pretty much to myself. My father's visits were brief; he worked until noon on Saturday, and could not reach Meredith until after dark on Saturday night; he left again after dinner on Sunday, by two thirty or three.

Mother slept late in the mornings. I was an early riser, my grandparents even earlier. My bedroom was above the kitchen, and I would wake to the sound of pots banging in the sink and my grandmother singing—"Bringing in the Sheaves," "Work for the Night Is Coming," "Seeing Nellie Home." At half-past six, my grandparents and I would eat breakfast in the dining room—oranges cut in half and sprinkled with white sugar, oatmeal with brown sugar and butter and cream, bacon, boiled eggs, cocoa, coffee, cinnamon toast. Until ten or so, when my mother awoke, I played in the yard or on the porch. If it was raining I played in the music room or the library—small rooms off the front hall, one with a piano and one with sets of books in glass-doored cases. My mother had breakfast in bed, and I would have a second breakfast with her. Then, when she was up and dressed, she came down to the music room and our lessons began.

They were hardly lessons, except for arithmetic and spelling. We were studying the myths and legends of Greece and Rome, and we took turns reading aloud from Hawthorne's *Wonder Book* and *Tanglewood Tales*. The stories I liked we read over and over again—Pandora's box, Perseus and Medusa, Midas and his daughter turned to gold, Ceres and Proserpine. Sometimes we took parts. I would play Epimetheus to my mother's Pandora, or Pluto to her Proserpine. We made peepshows in oatmeal boxes, to be looked at through a hole pricked in one end—Perseus holding high the snaky head, Pandora opening the forbidden box, dark Pluto upon his throne. Or we sat at the piano and made up songs about Ceres crying for her lost daughter, Midas boasting of his gold.

In the afternoons when the weather was fair we went walking, though not far and not for long—down Superior Street to the public library, or up Utica Street to a ravine about two blocks away. My mother dressed for our walks as if they were all-day outings, in her loose, wheat-colored coat, and her fox fur with jaws that snapped. I liked the ravine. It was one of several in Meredith, a town cut by small creeks that rise from pasture land to the south and empty into the Deer River, which empties into Lake Michigan. Where we went, the ravine was broad and shallow—it became deeper farther along—and a path led down an easy slope from Utica Street, across the creek on a wooden footbridge, and up the other side. Just off the path was a grassy clearing, and beneath a butternut tree there someone had set a green slatted bench that commanded a small prospect of the creek, the footbridge, and the upper ravine, where there were small fenced-off vegetable gardens. My mother liked to sit on the bench for an hour or so while I played. It was pleasant in the early afternoon, before school was out and the ravine became noisy with children. At that hour the place was our own.

Except for the clearing and the gardens above the bridge, the ravine grew wild; it was a tangle of sumac and scrub maple, wild grape, mulberry, barberry, and rosebushes gone to seed. To me it seemed a jungle, the dark unknown, as I thought it must have seemed to the first white men settling there—which, after all, had been less than a hundred years before. My imagination, fed and inflamed by the reading of myths and fairy tales, took root there and flowered. I saw spirits and demigods everywhere. Trolls lived beneath the footbridge. A hollow tree led to Pluto's kingdom, where dogs with eyes as big as cartwheels stood guard over his treasure. There were magic circles of toadstools in the clearing. The creek was a great sea, or the Styx, or the Nile. I began to tell such things to my mother—hesitantly at first, but she urged me on. Soon I was spinning fantastic tales—things I had long thought but never expected to say aloud; she would join in and carry me further. I had had the idea it was wrong to speak of such matters—imaginary playmates, winged horses, magic carpets, bogeymen. They weren't real. Yet here was my mother, who had been too busy or too nervous before to listen, not only allowing me to run on but running on herself. It was unheard of, and I felt there was something wrong in it. My mother was not supposed to be a child.

We began with stories and went on to plays, acting out our fantasies, half my mother's and half mine. Some of them were exciting enough to keep me awake, dreaming them over, at night. Once—it must have been late in April, for it was almost hot in the sun and my mother had taken off her coat—I was exploring the lower reaches of the ravine and came back to find her dozing on her bench.

"Hey," I said. "Wake up!"

She hushed me. "I'm the sleeping princess," she said. "I've been sleeping here for a thousand years."

"It's time you woke up," I said, before I saw that we were on the threshold of a new game. I had found a speckled brown-and-white eggshell and meant to ask her what bird's it was.

"Don't wake me harshly," my mother said. "It might be

fatal. A certain prince is to wake me and bring me back to life, but he must do it gently."

I knew the game then. "First I must perform certain tasks," I said.

We made them up. I would begin on the far side of the creek, at the top of the hill, and climb the small maple there (the dark tower, my mother said), then run down the path and cross the trolls' bridge—silently, or they would hear me and tear me to bits. Once safely across, I was to gather a bouquet of wild flowers and place them in my mother's hand.

"I have to go through the bramblebush first," I said. But my mother said no.

"Then I have to kiss you on the eyes," I said, and she agreed.

So it went. She was asleep, half seated and half lying, on the bench. I gave her a bouquet of white and purple violets and I kissed her, and she awoke, fluttering her eyelids, rising, yawning, and sitting erect to stretch and smile. I hopped about for joy at her surprise and my mastery.

We played the game again the next day, and it grew more elaborate. A dragon, she told me, had put her to sleep a thousand years before. He still lived in the culvert at the lower end of the ravine, and I must destroy him. I did, and came staggering back with his brown head, a heavy rock. Then we married—the ceremony was long, and each of us played several parts—and then I charged the bridge, screaming, and drove out all the trolls.

My mother went to the hospital early one morning toward the end of April, sooner than anyone expected. We had gone to the ravine just a day or so before. My father was in Chicago; no one was prepared. I felt at loose ends all that day. Late in the afternoon my father arrived, stopped just long enough to leave his bag and give me a glass jar of barley candy sticks, and went on to the hospital. He didn't come back for dinner. I was made to eat in the kitchen, alone, and sent up early to bed. I woke— it must have been around three in the morning—when he crawled into bed with me, wearing his BVDs. What was he doing in my bed? He always slept in Mother's room. I pulled the covers around me and pretended to be asleep. He lay flat with his hands at his sides, as if he were standing at attention on his back. He was shivering. I sat up and looked down at him, and he looked up at me as if he wondered who I was.

"You have a baby sister," he said, and began to chew at the knuckles of his right hand. "She's dead," he said. I thought he meant my sister. "Your mother is dead," he said, and put his fist in his mouth. I didn't know what he meant.

There were noises in the kitchen, and I went down by the back stairs to see what was going on. My grandmother and my grandfather sat there drinking tea. I wanted to ask them what my father was talking about; I guessed him to mean my mother was very tired and worn out from having my sister. My notions of birth, like my notions of death, were imprecise, but I knew that giving birth meant pain. "Is Mommy all right?" I said.

My grandmother said yes, she was out of her suffering. My grandfather said nothing. I sat down, and my grandmother poured me some warm tea and milk.

"Why is Daddy sleeping in my bed?" I said.

"Hush, Bobby," my grandfather said.

"We'll talk about it in the morning," my grandmother said. "It's the middle of the night."

My grandfather took me back to my bedroom by the front stairs. In the upstairs hall, there was a cedar chest. We sat down on it, and he told me what had happened.

"Your sister's name is Helen Marie," he said. "She is a fine, healthy baby, and she will have brown eyes and brown hair just like you and your mother. A few hours after the baby was born, Ruth—your mother—passed away in her sleep. Your father talked to her before she died, and so did your grandmother and I. She saw the baby and said she wanted to call her Helen Marie, and then we left her alone to sleep. She was tired, but she was well. Then a clot of blood formed and went to her heart and killed her. Her heart stopped beating. There was nothing any of us could do—" He checked himself then, as if he had been talking to someone else and I had just walked into the room. His voice had trembled. I felt embarrassed. And I could not quite believe him; I felt he was telling me a story and not all the truth, for reasons I did not understand. I did not think my mother was dead.

I woke late the next morning with the feeling that there was something I had to do; I could not remember what it was. My father was gone. When I got to the kitchen, my breakfast was on the table and my grandmother sat at the kitchen counter, polishing silverware. The sun was high enough to shine through the walnut tree in the back yard and into the kitchen windows. Flecks of greenish light and shadow were on the white enamel table and on my breakfast. I was in a hurry to get outside.

"Don't bolt your food, Robert," my grandmother said. "I want to talk to you." She sat down beside me, so that I could not see her face clearly.

My mother had passed away, she told me, but she was not dead. We should think of her as asleep. We would see her again, and we would all be together one day. She was waiting for us now in Heaven.

"Can she see us?" I said.

Yes, she could see us. She was watching us, and waiting.

I could see her, wearing a white robe, holding on to the gold gateposts of Heaven and leaning out, looking down through the clouds. I wanted to ask if she had wings.

Here was another story, like my grandfather's, but this was one I thought I could understand and believe. My grandmother's voice was firm, and what she told me was no more than what I already knew. Mother was not really dead; my father, though he wept and bit his fist, must have been wrong. I let my grandmother hold me for a moment, and went out to play.

Dying, in the Bishop family, was no more to be talked about freely than other natural functions. Mourning was brief, and the children were usually spared. I did not attend my mother's funeral or her burial, or see her dead. After that morning there was no more talk of her death in my hearing. Early in the afternoon my father took me over to his father's house, and I stayed there for three days, helping my other grandfather tend his chickens and paint his truck, while the body of my mother lay (unknown to me) before the glazed green tile fireplace in the Bishops' living room. I knew, surely, that I was being kept out of the way for her funeral, but I didn't know why. I did not return to the Bishop house until the day after her burial in the family plot in the cemetery at Corinth, ten miles away.

When my father came for me it was not to take me with him back to Chicago. He had talked things over with my grandmother and the Doctor, he told me, and they all thought it would be better if Helen Marie and I stayed on with the Bishops for a while. It was almost summer, soon it would be hot, there was more room in Meredith, and we would have better care. By fall, he'd find someone to keep house for us in Chicago, and everything would work out all right. He left me at the Bishops' and drove back to the city.

A week or so later Helen Marie came back from the hospital. A nurse, Miss Rutledge, brought her. They took my mother's old room, and Miss Rutledge stayed on, sleeping next to the crib. My sister nearly died in her first few weeks at home. She had no wet nurse, and none of the formulas worked. She came down with croup. The house stank of sour vomit and diapers, and echoed with her angry crying. My youngest aunt, Aunt Elda, came home to live, quitting her job in Ann Arbor. The kitchen became a laboratory, the counters and the en-

amelled table cluttered with beakers, scales, and cans of Dex-
tromalt, Karo syrup, powdered milk. Everything in the house
went toward keeping the baby alive. I was left out—hurried
through breakfast, dinner, and supper, and shooed away to play.
I felt sapped of life, as if it were being transferred from me into
that raging, insatiable monster. I hated her; if it weren't for her
coming, my mother would still have been there.

Then one day Helen Marie was well and Miss Rutledge
left. My sister lay in her buggy in the side yard each morning,
taking the sun. We opened windows and put up the porch
screens. People came to call. We went for drives along the lake
shore in the evening. My father came nearly every weekend,
and he stayed for two weeks in July. He gave me a back-yard
gym and a camera. We drove to the Corinth cemetery, where he
showed me my mother's grave. There was no sign of the burial;
the plot had been sodded and the grass was dark green. By mid-
summer, my grandmother, who wore black for the first months,
let herself be persuaded by Aunt Elda to put on her flowered
summer frocks again.

I was giving little thought to my mother's absence. The details of a new, busy life filled my days and sent me to bed tired
at night. I made friends with the Keller boys, who were visiting
for the summer at a house up Utica Street, and I introduced
them to the ravine, where we played rougher games than my
mother and I had played. Old Mr. Keller, their grandfather, was
a wholesale grocer; we cadged wooden boxes from him and built
a clubhouse in their barn. I was seldom home.

The Bishop family was taking my mother's loss calmly, or so
it appeared. Aunt Nora—she was Roman Catholic, married to
my father's brother—thought me an unfeeling child and the
Bishops heathens for paying so little respect to the dead. Yet
each Sunday, when my father came from Chicago, we drove to
Corinth to visit Mother's grave. We brought fresh flowers from
the garden for the spiked green tin vases stuck in the ground by

the new headstone. The Bishop plot was large and held a dozen graves; there were shrubs in the corners and beds of flowers along the edges. My grandmother and Aunt Elda tended the beds, transplanting new flowers from the garden at home, while my sister lay in her wicker basket near them and my father and Dr. Bishop, talking, walked up and down the cemetery paths. With garden shears, I clipped at the long grass that the caretaker's mower missed until I tired of work and went off to play. The cemetery was large and hilly, and I would run up and down hill, threading in and out among the graves. We were successfully domesticating her death.

Our visits to the cemetery came to be as familiar and as natural as our visits, often during the same afternoon, to my great-aunts and cousins in Corinth who were still alive. My mother's death and her lying buried there came to seem natural, too, as natural as spring giving way to summer and summer to fall. And yet, though I understood that my mother's body lay in the Corinth cemetery, I still had the feeling, supported by what my grandmother had said of Heaven, that she was alive. It was a feeling I kept to myself.

Now and then I felt her presence—not as a ghost, not anything I could sense. She seemed to be with me, but just on the other side of a tough, clouded membrane that neither she nor I could pierce. And a few times I felt her more intimately, in some buoyancy of spirit, or in a sharp, momentary recollection of my well-being before her death, or in the occasional will to be well or to do well that sprang up inside me just when I was at my worst. And once, late in August, I thought I saw her ghost— thinking at the same time that it was an illusion. I was standing outside the Bishop house, leaning against one of the pair of catalpas planted beside the front walk. It was a cool evening, and getting on toward dark. The front-porch light and the lights in the living room had not yet been turned on, and my grandmother and Aunt Elda had gone to visit old Mrs. Carnes, who lived next door. My grandfather was out on a call. Through the large window of the music room I saw a figure in white pause in the doorway to the room, as if listening or looking for something, one hand raised to turn on the light. But no light went on, and after a moment the figure withdrew, as if satisfied that everything was in order. It had to be my grandmother or my aunt—coming back, perhaps, for a shawl—yet I shivered.

In the fall my loneliness overtook me. I looked around, and saw that my mother had indeed gone for good and that my father had left my sister and me to be raised by people who were gray and old. I had been advanced another year to the sixth grade, skipping the fifth, which meant that the boys in my class were all a good two years older and stronger than I. I found myself first in class in studies—I didn't have the cunning to play dumb—and last in sports. I gave up sports. The Keller boys had gone, and after school I'd go down to the ravine, or hang around my room, or go off to the public library. I became a bookworm. I brought home six books at a time and went through two a day. "This is our walking encyclopedia," my grandfather said.

The librarian was kind and took me for a prodigy. I may have been, but I dissipated my gifts. Though I read the proper books she gave me, it was with none of the ardor with which I turned to books I took from the adult shelves and kept hidden in the children's room behind bound volumes of *St. Nicholas Magazine*. I discovered a taste for horror. Rohmer, Wallace, Poe, books on witches, voodoo, prisons, executions, hospitals, plagues, volcanic eruptions, earthquakes, tidal waves, grave robbers, cadavers, wars—I gourmandized them all. Nothing could frighten me enough. The books were weak things, but I got from them what I needed to frame fantasies of my own. There was a reason for this, of course; I know that now. I told myself tales to keep from thinking of what was worse—my abandonment, my mother's death. I lay in bed and saw Chinese pirates, hatchets raised, creep out of secret panels in my walls. The laundry chute in the hall next to my bedroom hid monsters. Falling asleep, I saw the ceiling descend upon me slowly, and I started up, panting. Asleep, I woke from dreams in which someone or something just outside my window was rapping, crying to be let in. I had nightmares. I was covered with boils that burst, and out of them came snakes, mice, bats, and little cursing black men.

Odd sensations began to come over me. Lying in bed one night, I felt my big toes growing—growing until they felt like potatoes. It was ridiculous, but I was afraid to look at them. They were the *wrong size,* they would have to be cut off. I couldn't bear the thought. I wiggled them, and they felt bigger, and then the feeling passed and I fell asleep. But the illusion returned from time to time, until I lay awake waiting for it, stiff with anxiety. I was frightened; it was something over which I had no control.

Later in the year—it would have been November or December, for the grass in the park I cut through on the way to school was tipped with frost—I was assailed by something, not so much a sensation as the lack of it, that frightened me more. I was late for school, the first bell had already rung, and I was hurrying through the little park (it was only a block square), running over in my head a poem I had memorized and was to recite before the class. I had chosen it myself; it was by Eugene Field, the stanzas were short, and the story concerned a boy and girl who died from eating green peaches. I was halfway through the poem and halfway through the park, walking quickly, when I felt my heart slow and my senses and my brain stop dead, though everything outside me was going on just the same. I seemed to be in another world, as if I were a ghost, as if I were enclosed by glass. In that state, wherever it was, everything seemed to be whirring and disconnected, like stripped

gears. Wheels in my head, and wheels outside. I was choking
with impatience and disgust; it was as if the firmament had
cracked and through it I could see chaos. And then the world
came flooding back. It had only been a few seconds; I had gone
on walking, and I was nearly across the park. The brick school
was just before me, with knotted, leafless vines of ivy snaking
across its face. The tardy-bell began to ring, slowly. I hurried.
Above me, there was a flurry of sparrows. I looked back from
the steps. Everything was where it should be, looking new.

That experience of dislocation or estrangement—whatever
it was—returned often, but only when I was alone and out-of-
doors. By late fall, I was going to the public library even more,
for in that place, so full of promises and distractions and fabri-
cated terrors, I was set free from my own fears. And there was
company in the library, too. Anyone could enter—people of
whom my grandmother disapproved, people we would never
have in the house: Mincing Walter, who dressed in checked
suits and lived with his sister; Jerry Morris, the tongue-tied boy,
whom we called "Dewwy Mahwiss," and who tried to read aloud
to himself in the library; the river-bottom Irish; Negroes; serv-
ants; strangers; farmers; Jews. Their leavings were among the
oily pages of the popular novels. I found crumbs, flowers, letters,
lists, hairs, ink blots, pins, and pencilled vituperations in them.
The library first gave me what I discovered later in amusement
parks, resorts, museums, transcontinental trains—a promiscuous
society in which I could be silent, secret, and free, enclosed and
sustained by unknown possibilities, and where there was the
promise, always, of finding again what I had lost.

My dread, though, was becoming too great to be contained
for long, and I began to fear common things—the night, sudden
noises, blood, footsteps in the dark, waiting for someone. I seldom went to the ravine now. It made me uneasy—even the
clearing where my mother and I used to play. To get to the library, I passed the ravine at another place, where Superior

Street crossed it on a fill. The ravine was wilder and deeper there than where we had played, and frightening to me near dusk and after. The sidewalk was of rough concrete, the kind that jars a roller skater's teeth and joints, and it had been tipped and buckled in several places by the roots of trees. Between it and the drop into the ravine, there was only a double-railed, whitewashed fence. Below was a tangle of brush and brambles. When I was three, I had been told the bogeyman lived there. Now I thought of tramps and gypsies and wild beasts. The creek moved more swiftly at that point, and disappeared into a corrugated-iron culvert to pass under the street to the other side. In dry months, the culvert could be crawled through; I went into it one day and out the other side, carrying a flashlight, on a dare from the Keller boys. The headless corpse of a girl had been found there once, we had heard. I found nothing but slime, sticky cobwebs, stink, and excrement. Where the street crossed the ravine, it seemed to grow dark half an hour before it was dark in the rest of the town, and walking there at dusk was like crossing a narrow bridge over a black pool from which the blackness might rise to overwhelm you. In summer, spiders threw threads across the way to tickle the nostrils and earholes, and I learned to walk with my hands pawing before me, like a man gone blind. An owl lived in the great oak that rose from the ravine floor and towered above the elms that lined the street. There were bats in the evening, and after a rain earthworms on the sidewalk would squish underfoot.

During the winter, though, there seemed less to fear. Unleaved trees offered no hiding place, and snow changed the ravine, covering its thickets and briars, levelling its contours, and lightening its darkness. I minded the walk less, and began to forget I had been afraid. Snow packed hard on the path across the troll bridge, and I'd sled there after school until suppertime. I was good enough at that, and soon I found myself one of a gang.

By late winter I was becoming my grandparents' child. Nothing came of my father's plans to bring my sister and me back to Chicago. He had been able to drive to Meredith each weekend while the weather held, but now he could come less often on the icy roads. I began to draw close to my grandfather. He was gentle, or he had become gentle; he could not speak sharply to me. Of him, now, I remember only glimpses. He stands before the mirror in the upstairs bathroom and spreads Burma-Shave on his face; his thick mustache is as white as the shaving cream. He comes home late from a call and tears bits of bread into a bowl for his bread and milk. He introduces me to the president of the First Bank of Meredith, a very old man who wears a gray sweater under his coat; the president's father was the first white man to set foot in Meredith, I am told. "How could he tell it was Meredith, then?" I am supposed to have said. And now I see my grandfather playing croquet at dusk in the yard; he is in shirtsleeves, and his shirt shines white. Moles have undermined the lawn—their tunnels are everywhere—and the croquet balls go comically astray.

My grandmother, worried by my brooding, did what she could to keep me out of mischief; she called my mother to her aid. Mother was watching me day and night, she told me over and over. Mother was praying that I would be good, so that I could join her one day. Whenever I did anything bad, Mother saw me. Wherever I was, there was no hiding from her. She knew.

I only half believed such stories, but they weighed on my soul. What if they were true? What if I were to miss out on Heaven because I didn't brush my teeth at night? What if, through some such foolish omission, I never saw my mother again? It was safer to be good, and I became a good boy, except for the times when a burst of anger or high spirits carried me away, and except for my thoughts, which I thought invisible. I became overscrupulous. I washed my hands five times before meals and appeared at table with clenched fists to keep out the germs. I knew little of the gradations of sin or forgiveness. I saw gold stars and black marks in the book of life, and nothing in between. I behaved, and my imagination continued to grow rank and wild.

By springtime, my mother had firmly assumed her place in Heaven—a Gothic figure, smiling severely, as stiff as her body in its grave. When I thought of her, it was there in Heaven beside the recording angel, or in the Corinth cemetery; I felt her presence no longer. Neither was I conscious of her loss, and memories of her alive were passing from my mind. My father, too, was receding; he had his place in Chicago now, my distant benefactor. Only when he was about to come to Meredith or about to leave did I feel our old ties. I was little trouble to anyone, and no one knew what was on my mind. I had turned to thinking of death, my mother's and my own, and although I could not conceive of being dead, I liked to imagine my dying, and I hoped to die while I could still be good and there was still a chance of Heaven.

In the attic of the Bishop house, I found the skeleton of a child, a girl of twelve or so, brought home by my grandfather from medical school and forgotten. It was packed in a wooden box with a sliding lid. Its bones were articulated, and it could be lifted out and hung, by a ring set in its skull, from a metal stand. It was beautiful. The child had been small—I was told years later she was Chinese—and she was about my height. I could feel with my fingertips the curve of her pelvic bone, the smooth tibia, the prick of her fingers, the hollows of her eyes. I would think of her dying and of the slow vanishing of her flesh. Then I thought of it happening to my mother, and that it would one day happen to me. Whatever the truth about Heaven might be, the softness of the body and the hardness of bone were sure. Lying under the covers of my bed in the dark, I cupped a hand over my flashlight and saw my own bones shadowed there in pink, translucent flesh. I found comfort in that, and in the child's skeleton, and discovered I was not so much afraid.

One Saturday in April, when Helen Marie was nearly a year old, my aunt went off to visit a girl friend in Grand Rapids for the weekend, and my grandmother suddenly took it into her head, early in the afternoon, to drive over to Corinth and visit her sister. My father could not come that weekend, and I was sulking. I didn't want to go to visit Aunt Sallie, and my grandmother—wonder of wonders—let me stay behind. Off she went, with the baby bundled in the wicker basket on the seat beside her. I was on my way to the library before they were out of the drive. I had found a new obsession, the tales of Robert Louis Stevenson, and was reading them straight through. They seemed charged with some kind of forbidden energy, and I was excited by them without knowing why.

When I returned home hungry about five-thirty, I found my grandfather, just back from his office, there alone. Grandma wouldn't be home until tomorrow, so we were bachelors, he said. She and Aunt Sallie had got to talking and she had decided to spend the night. She had called to tell him there was cold ham loaf in the icebox and potato soup on the stove, and she had made a spice cake that morning. We ate in the kitchen, put the dishes in the sink, and were settling down to a game of casino when the phone rang. It was the city hospital. Two out-of-town cars had collided on Deadman's Curve; at least six people were badly hurt; they needed him right away.

My grandfather drove off, and I went back to the library, having promised to be home and in bed before dark. I stayed too late, of course, until the lights flicked off and on just before closing, at ten minutes to nine. It was nearly dark. How had it got so late? I plopped Stevenson into his hiding place behind the bound volumes of *St. Nicholas* and set out for home. The sky, fortunately, was not yet black. (In that part of Michigan, our clocks were well over an hour ahead of sun time.) I ran, cutting across the library lawn, then past the telephone building and the low Christian Science church, past old Mr. Kane's brick house, across Troy Street, past the Tennyson Club, and down toward the ravine, where my old fears returned to assail me. I can still recall it, to this day. The street is empty. A light suspended between two poles casts shadows that move with the wind. Something down in the ravine crackles in the quiet. It is only a hundred long steps to home, but I cannot make it. Someone—a tramp, or gypsy—is waiting for me, ready to force me into the ravine. Something brushes my ear, or I think it does, and I turn and run, back to the long, safe way home. Circling the ravine by roads where the street lights are brightest, I run, down Troy Street, past the Simpsons', Browns', Burgers', Kendalls', Stricklands'—all houses I know. There is light on Troy Street still; the houses sit well back from the sidewalk, and the sky is open to the west. I decide to cut through the ravine after all—the other way, across the footbridge—and come home by the back door. The ravine is broader there, and open enough to be light.

I wait, catch my breath, and begin to trot. Around the corner toward the ravine, past the Nelsons'. Mr. Nelson is busy with his car in the garage; his headlights go on, dim, but brighter than the purple air. He waves. I wave back and run on, on to the end of the sidewalk and the cinder path that dips into the ravine. The footing is worse than I expected; the spring rains have cut gullies in the path—miniature ravines leading to the creek, which has become a swollen miniature river. Near the bottom, the cinders have washed away, leaving slick orange clay, and I slip and fall. It is not much of a fall. I have twisted my ankle, though, and now I must go slowly.

But at the bottom of the ravine it has grown dark, as black

as the bottom of a lake. My ankle hurts and I sit on the railing of the footbridge to ease it. A minute ago it seemed to be light. When had it become dark? I begin to speculate—too busily to be afraid. What was the moment of the change? When I fell? When my knees hit the ground? My knickers are soaked through at the knees, and I feel the cold. Where was the split second before which it was light and after which it was dark? Or is it all in the mind, and "dark" and "light" only what somebody calls things, and everything no more than a great whirr, with the names all wrong and the world merely one cell in some great dark being that stretches past the stars? The objects around me begin to flow away, and once more that feeling of dislocation overcomes me and I seem to take leave of my body and senses.

In a moment or two, my sensations begin to return—I am still sitting on the bridge—and first comes the sensation of smell. But mixed with the smell of wet clay from the ravine comes something else: honey-and-almond, peppermint, tea, cold cream, linseed oil, and cloves—my mother's smells, coming to me singly and then together. Presently I can taste as well, and then I can hear and see. The ravine comes to life in the dark, full of hidden shapes, like one of those leafy puzzle drawings in which are to be found ponies, or kittens, or Ali Baba and his thieves. But the shapes in the ravine are unfamiliar and nameless, seemingly in motion though I cannot catch them moving. Their turbulence is gentle, like the oily surface of a river backwater, and is somehow just out of sight; from them comes a sharp humming, almost too high-pitched to hear. I am frightened almost to death. But then there comes to me the strong sense of my mother's presence, for the first time in many months. This time, though, she is *outside*. I have something more than the old inward awareness of her. I can see nothing, but I *know she is there*. I should be afraid, but I am not, and I walk slowly, favoring my ankle, feeling my mother beside me still, across the bridge and up the easy slope until the appearances in the ravine are behind me. The way home, once

I reach the street, is well lighted. A ball game has just broken up in the park nearby, and I hear the boys crying good night, and the crack, crack of a baseball bat striking the pavement.

I went up to the house by the back way and, puzzling out how to explain my lateness to my grandfather, let myself in. The doors were never locked. The back porch was dark; so were the pantry and the kitchen. Clicking lights on as I went, I walked through the back hall to the front of the house. Dark, except for the porch light outside. The house was empty; the Doctor wasn't home yet. What a relief! The large clock in the hall whirred, paused, clicked, and struck. Ten o'clock? I counted nine, then looked at its face. Nine o'clock. I had left the library only ten minutes before; I was hardly late at all. With luck, I would be in bed before my grandfather came.

It was quiet, though, with the house empty—and exciting, as if I were a spy in enemy territory. I had never been alone for long in the house at night. I felt victorious. I had not been afraid in the ravine; I could not show fear now. I sat down on the stairs and listened. Only the clock, with its halting tick, tock-tick, tock-tick, like an old man limping. A car going by outside, the beams of its lights sweeping the living room as far as the green tile fireplace. The living room in shadow, antimacassars on the dark-brown chairs and sofa showing palely. Someone walking outside, turning the corner. Coming here? No, turning the corner. Someone going home. Upstairs, there was no sound. My bedroom was up there in the back of the house. How was I to get upstairs and into bed, and turn out the lights behind me, and not be in the dark? I wanted my grandfather to find me asleep, with the downstairs in darkness, as if I had gone to bed before night. Ah, yes. There was a way. I turned on the light in the upstairs hall by the switch at the foot of the stairs. Then I went back to the pantry and came through the kitchen again, switch-

ing off the lights behind me. Leaving a dim lamp on in the front
hall, I went quickly up the stairs, through the hall, and to my
room before there was time to think of what might possibly be
behind the other bedroom doors. And now, in bed, I felt safe.

Not for long. I had counted on the Doctor's coming right
home. I would hear his car in the driveway; the car door would
close, and then the back door, and my grandfather would come
up the stairs and find me asleep. "Robert, are you playing pos-
sum?" he would say, and I might sit up in bed and say yes, and
where had he been? But he didn't come, and he didn't come.
Where was he? Had he gone to the scene of the accident, to
Deadman's Curve, and been killed there himself? I could see
him lying among the bloody, contorted corpses, a car overturned just behind them, one wheel spinning.

The phone rang, bringing bad news. I could not answer; it
would mean going out into the black hall. I let it ring, and lay
there, counting the rings. Twelve times. Thirteen. Fourteen.
Then nothing, though I heard ringing still in the empty house.
Then there was nothing at all, and I lay stiff in my bed, hands
on my belly, trying not to give in to my anxiety. A few weeks before, I had invented horrors and sought out fear. Now I was
tired; I had had enough. Yet as I lay in bed with my eyes shut,
straight as a stick, the covers up to my chin, images came un-
summoned to my eyes. A bearded shepherd who held a ram on
a leash, straining to break free. A drowned girl with staring eyes.
A plane diving at me, its machine gun blazing. I could not get
past the images, across the threshold to sleep. It would be better
to stay awake.

I got up and dressed again, and went through the house
turning on all the lights. In the bedrooms, closets, bathrooms.
The ceiling lights and the bridge lamps and the table lamps in
the living room, the music room, and the library. The kitchen

lights and the lights on the porches, back and front. The garage lights, which turned on from the back pantry, and the light above the sign in the front yard, reading, in gilt on black, "AN-DREW BISHOP, M.D." I turned on the cellar lights from the head of the stairs, and locked and bolted the cellar doors. Remembering the skeleton, I went upstairs once more and locked the door to the attic. I locked the front door, the side door, the back door. I switched on the radio, found a dance band, and turned it up high. I remembered the dining-room chandelier and turned it on, and then I went back to the radio and danced, screaming out the words to songs I knew, or making up my own.

My grandfather had to ring the front-door bell to get in. It woke me. He had not been killed after all; several people had been badly hurt in the accident, he told me, and he had been in the hospital operating room, working with a surgeon, for hours. I had fallen asleep, finally, with the radio still on, and dreamed that all of us were sitting in the living room listening to the music—my mother and father, Aunt Sallie and Uncle Ben from Corinth, both my grandmothers, both my grandfathers, Aunt Nora and Uncle John (my father's brother), my aunts and my uncle on my mother's side, and my sister Helen Marie, who was grown. My mother got up to go to bed and kissed each of us good night. She came last to me and bent over—I was still my own size—and I kissed her on the cheek. I knew what no one else there knew, that she would die in the night, and for some reason I could not tell, or show my feeling. I could only kiss her good night. I woke from the dream into the brightly lit living room—I was lying on the sofa—and then fell asleep again, just before my grandfather came and woke me to come to the door.

He stood in the doorway and looked down at me.

"I put on all the lights," I said. "I was worried."

He turned off the radio, sat me down on the sofa, and sat down beside me. He felt my hands, and then he felt my forehead with his wrist. He smelled of ether. "What is it, Bobby?" he said. "You're as pale as a ghost."

What was I to tell him? I could not tell him the truth about what had happened in the ravine, or about the fear that assailed me when I got back inside the house. It would shame me, and besides, I hadn't the words. I would have to tell him a story. I told him I had come through the ravine and I had found my mother's ghost there, sitting on the bench where she used to sit, and she had risen and come toward me.

"You've been seeing things," he said. "There aren't any ghosts."

"I *saw* her," I insisted. "She was sitting on the bench, and then she got up and began to walk." I could see her more clearly as I spoke. "She was carrying a baby," I said.

"That's enough, Bobby," my grandfather said.

"She was carrying a baby, and she walked toward me, very slowly. One of her legs was dragging. She was dressed all in white, and her hair was down, and there was blood running down her front." I would *make* him believe me.

My grandfather had got up, but now he sat down heavily on the sofa beside me. "It was only your imagination," he said. "You have to put it out of your mind."

"I only saw her for a minute," I said. "Then she said something and went away."

"What was it?" my grandfather said. He was interested.

"It was 'Come back, come back!' " I said.

He was silent, and then he took me up to my bed and sat with me until I fell asleep.

My grandfather woke me at six the next morning, his usual hour. I could smell coffee, and bacon frying. I wanted to stay in bed, but he pulled off the covers and made me get up. After breakfast we walked down to the ravine, taking the back way, the way I had come the night before. It was chilly. The sun was not yet high enough to reach into the ravine, and dew hung from the grass. We found wild flowers in the clearing and along the creek, and I told my grandfather their names. My mother had taught them to me the year before—spring beauties, trillium, bloodroot, adder's-tongues. During the World War, he told me, the neighborhood children had planted a vegetable garden in the clearing. My mother, a girl then, was in command of the project. There were stringbeans, carrots, beets, and spring onions. The rabbits had taken them all. They were not patriotic rabbits, my mother had said.

We walked over to the bench under the butternut tree and sat down. He turned and pointed to a rag caught on a bush just back of the bench. "That must be what you saw last night," he said. "It was just a fluttering rag, and you imagined the rest." He took the rag from the bush and stuffed it into his overcoat pocket. Everything around us seemed natural to me, and in its right place again. What had I been thinking of to lie to him the night before?

He sat, his hands upon his knees, and looked at me. "I haven't been down here in years," he said. "Your mother used to come here often when she was a little girl. She would run away and hide here, and I would come down to find her."

I nodded.

"Your mother was our first child," he said. "We loved her very much. I can't tell you why she had to die so young, but there was nothing we could do."

"We will see her in Heaven," I said.

He nodded. "There was nothing I could have done," he said. "And she was my own daughter."

I looked up at him. How strange! How strange that I had never thought of that before. My mother was Grandpa Bishop's daughter. He was her father, I was her son. He had lost her, too. My father had lost her, and my sister. And my mother had lost her life and lost us all.

"Your mother is buried in the Corinth cemetery," my grandfather said. "That is where my father and mother are buried, and where your grandmother and I will be buried someday— and where you may be, too, if you want to be, when it comes your turn. Your mother's body lies there, and her soul is in Heaven. I don't want to hear any more talk of ghosts."

"Of course not. I promise," I said. "There was never any ghost. That was only a story."

Circles

Late one summer afternoon in a bar off Greenwich Avenue Frank Hale encountered his wife, Julie, from whom he had been separated for half a year. She was waiting, she told him, for her new beau. Frank bought her a Scotch and they talked to each other reasonably, as they always had, about their son Timmy, now going on seven, who was away at camp, and about their jobs and families. After a while Frank found he had no more to say and sat making circles with the bottom of his glass on the bar. He felt himself entering one of the long silences that had come over him since their separation, and he saw Julie looking at him with concern. "What is it?" she said.

Wetting a forefinger in his Scotch, Frank drew a circle before him and then another, a smaller one that barely intersected the first. "The people I see only touch me on a small arc like this," he said, looking down at what he had drawn. "I need more people. I need enough to touch me all around." He quickly drew circles like toothless gears around the circle in the center that stood for himself.

"Are you sleeping with anyone?" Julie asked.

"Sure," Frank said. "It's not that." Julie was sure to think of that solution first. Not that he was sleeping with anyone. Not that it wasn't partly that.

Julie, who was very pretty and very myopic, leaned over to

examine what Frank had drawn. Her hair, a brighter red than he remembered, fell over one eye; she raised her head and looked straight at him while she pushed back her hair. Oh God, Frank thought. Her hair had always fallen over her eye and she was always pushing it back, looking earnestly at people, and explaining things. For nine years he had been looked at earnestly through those moist gray eyes.

"None of your circles reach the center," Julie said.

"They can't," Frank said. "You never reach the center."

"You *do*," Julie said, and put her hand on his. "You do, Frank. *We* did." That was true. Or they had thought they had. They used to read e. e. cummings to each other—

> (*with a spin*
> *leap*
> *alive we're alive*)
> *we're wonderful one times one.*

On the inside of their matching wedding bands was engraved the equation $1 \times 1 = 1$, and hadn't that meant that they were one, that they were one flesh? That together they were complete? He had once thought they were complete. He had *felt* complete.

Julie drew two closely overlapping circles before her, then rubbed them out and drew two that were nearly contiguous, like the illustration of an eclipse. She looked at Frank again. "It can be like this," she said.

"Oh," said Frank, hoping he did not sound bitter. "You're in love."

Julie nodded several times and smiled. She had been in love with Frank, and she had been in love with others during most of the years of their marriage; she had been in love with still others, he supposed, in the six months of their separation. For all he knew, she loved most of them still. For all he knew, she loved Hal still. She had principles and she held to them; she slept only with men she loved. "It's one of your infatuations," he said. "It's all in your mind."

Julie shook her head slowly from side to side. "I'm sorry, Frank," she said, her eyes brimming. "When you love you reach the center. It's the simple truth."

Frank got down off his bar stool and paid the check. "You want your life to be a series of highs, and I understand that," he said. "I wanted our life to be an unbroken chain."

A few weeks later, Julie met Frank in the apartment on Gramercy Park he had sublet from a girl in his office—Frank worked for one of the large charitable foundations—who had taken a summer's leave of absence and gone to Greece. It had been Julie's idea for them to meet. Or had it been Frank's? He couldn't remember. They were going to decide what to do with their marriage. The apartment was filled with low couches, Danish rugs, avocado plants, Japanese lanterns, and ticking clocks. Frank had promised the girl in the office that he would keep the plants watered and the clocks wound, a promise that pinned him down to the city through the summer. It was typical of his distorted sense of responsibility, Frank thought. Not that he wanted to go away.

After two drinks, without quite intending to, Frank went to bed with his wife. "It's just like adultery!" she cried happily as she took off her clothes. "And it's legal!" Frank wondered whether he was now the betrayer instead of the betrayed. Where was Julie's lover? Would she be seeing him later? Would she tell him? The evening was hot and close, and Frank lay down with Julie, naked, on a couch by a window in the green shade of the avocado plants massed on the sill above them. They embraced. It was not yet dark. This is the nuptial embrace,

Frank thought. Alas, he still desired his wife, and she desired him. He listened to the clocks ticking as he moved within her, and then he heard them no longer, and then, hearing them again, he returned reluctantly to Julie and to his life.

While Julie, still naked, was scrambling eggs in the narrow kitchen, Frank heard her sob. He edged in behind her and kissed the nape of her neck. She laughed her embarrassed laugh. "It's so *satisfactory* with you, that's all," she said. "It was like that the night you left."

"That's not why I left," Frank said. Not that he was sure why he had left. They had almost always got on in bed. It wasn't that. And it wasn't only that Julie slept around. If it were that simple, he would have left long before. He had always known of her lovers. Julie would tell him. How could she help telling him, she would ask; she and Frank had been too close for too long. She would try to keep each affair to herself, but at some point toward the end, usually after she and Frank had made satisfactory love, the need to talk would come over her and she would have to explain everything, all that had happened, and where, and her motives and the man's and how it had been in bed. These weren't confessions, exactly. Julie did not question her motives or speak of guilt or ask to be forgiven. What was there to forgive? She had been moved by love; she *believed* in love. She loved Frank. She *had* to share her experience with him—didn't they always tell each other everything? —and she had to analyze it all, and explain.

Julie's first adventure had been in the third year of their marriage, and Frank had listened quietly while she told him about it. He had been surprised and hurt, but at the end of her account he heard himself saying no more than, "Yes, yes, I understand, of course I understand." What else should he have said? He had been brought up to be kind to women. And what was the point in getting angry? Or in threatening to leave? He didn't want to leave. She didn't want him to leave. He loved

Julie and he loved his new son. They all loved each other. And these things pass.

But they did not pass. And what reason had he to protest Julie's third or fourth or seventh adventure when he had condoned the ones before? And why should Julie hide anything from him? Hadn't he given her her freedom? There was a period when she became impatient with him, with his doglike fidelity and his indifference to other women. He was being unfair, she told him. It wasn't enough for her to be free alone; he had to be free, too, or they would never feel equal and the unbalance would destroy their marriage. He tried. He went to bed with the girl he'd been sleeping with when he and Julie met, though it gave neither him nor the girl any pleasure. When he told Julie, she burst into tears. Not because he had been "unfaithful"—there was no such thing—but because he had made love without love. How could he go to bed with that *tramp?* She had given him credit for better taste. He might at least pick women as good as she.

And so Frank slept only with Julie for five years, and their life flowed along, and they got on well enough with each other, and Timmy grew up with both mother and father at his side. And when Julie took a new lover she would eventually tell Frank about it and he would listen without saying much. And then one night in bed, as Julie began to tell him of still another lover, Frank got up, put on his clothes, and went away.

On the night of their reunion in the Gramercy Park apartment, the discussion Frank and Julie planned on having never took place. But she must want me back, Frank thought. What if she thinks now I *want* to come back? Unable to sleep for worry, he called her late the next night and, finding she was alone, walked over—she was living on East Twelfth Street, not far away—and told her that he meant their separation to be for good. "It's my turn to be free. That's a little joke," he said. All Julie said was, "I'm sorry, Frank. I truly am." Tears were in her eyes. What did she mean by saying she was sorry? Was this contrition? Whatever it was, it was too late. Frank told her that he wanted a formal separation right away. The words began to spill out of him. They should get divorced without dragging it out for years the way some people did, he said. And if they ever intended to start new lives, they'd better not sleep together. Not ever. Not ever again. Julie said nothing. Thank God, Frank thought as he left, there was no scene. He couldn't have held out if there had been a scene, if Julie had talked back, say, or said *anything*—said "Come here for a minute." They'd be in bed right now. He walked back to Gramercy Park up Second Avenue against a fitfully gusting wind, through eddies of dirt and torn papers. The moon, just past full, hung over Beth Israel Hospital, and for a moment made him think of the closely over-lapping circles of love that Julie had drawn that afternoon in the bar. Soon, he thought, he and Julie would be as far apart as the moon and the sun.

But he would continue to want her for a long time, he real-ized later that night after several drinks. Why was he leaving her if he still wanted her? Why did he want her if he couldn't stand her? Why couldn't he stand her? Because she asked so much of him? So much understanding, so much forbearance, so much indignity? But had either of them ever known how much to ask of the other, or even *what* to ask? Perhaps Julie didn't want to be "free" at all. Perhaps each time she took a lover she was really hoping he would draw the line. He didn't know. They had been swept into marriage by their passion when they were both so young, eighteen and twenty-three, when neither of them was formed or knew what moved them. Not that he knew now. Not that he knew anything now.

But hadn't *she* left him first—with that first lover, years ago? The muscles in his arms and hands tensed. That, right there and then, was the end of their wonderful one-times-one. That was when their separation actually, physically, took place, in the flesh, when another man's flesh entered his wife's. He and Julie had not been one since then. All he was doing now was making their separation public, bringing it out into the open after all these years. If either of them was ever to lead his own life, if they were ever to be truly free, didn't that have to be done? Hadn't he been right to do it? His heart began to lift. Now, at last, wasn't the painful part nearly over? What if he did still want her! Desires fade. He had begun to break free. He might lust after her still, but the day was not far off when he would no longer care for her at all.

The girl who had sublet her apartment to Frank came back from Greece, and he moved to a furnished apartment on Horatio Street, not far from the West Side Highway. It was a grubby, cramped, noisy place, and for weeks, as he had expected to, Frank fell into a depression and saw no one but Timmy, whom he dutifully took from Julie early on Saturday and kept through Sunday. Neither had much to say to the other. Frank would read aloud while Timmy sat on his lap, or they would play Parcheesi or Concentration or go to Central Park or to a movie. Or Timmy would play alone. Much of the time he would pretend he was a horse, and let Frank communicate with him only by whinnies and neighs. Often Timmy would refuse to understand anything at all. He still talked freely at home, Julie said; even when he was a horse, she had no trouble making him understand.

Frank began to find Timmy's weekly visits a burden. Wasn't it asking too much of him, after all? Julie no longer had a job; she was drawing unemployment, and now that he had signed the separation agreement and paid her regularly every week she had more money than he, a good deal more. He worked hard through the week and the weekends were his only free time. Why should Julie have her weekends free to spend with her lover? He began to call for Timmy less often. Julie did not object. Timmy was a great comfort to her, she said.

For Frank's thirty-second birthday, in late September, Timmy gave him a card he had drawn laboriously with Crayolas on manila paper. On it a waxy black horse grazed in a green field dotted with purple and red and blue flowers. An orange sun looked down upon the scene from a dark blue sky. Below the picture was printed in lead pencil a verse that seemed to Frank a message from a distant, no longer attainable country:

> *Horses and Sheep*
> *And Cattle and all*
> *Always always*
> *Come to my call.*

And I do not, Frank thought. And I cannot. Julie telephoned him at his office. "Happy birthday," she said. "Did you get Timmy's card? Isn't it *marvelous?* His teacher says that's his first serious attempt at communication in months."

I should be pleased, Frank thought. I should tell her that I am really pleased. But he could say nothing of the kind. It would be difficult enough thanking Timmy. Did they want him back? Did *she* want him back? Had she made up those lines? But no, that was absurd. The truth must be that Timmy, who he had thought was suffering more than either of them, had begun to recover. And Julie seemed happy enough. Why should it be so difficult for *me* to speak, Frank thought, and impossible for me to love?

While Timmy was riding a pony-cart in Central Park one Sunday in October, Frank saw a pretty woman detach herself from the parents grouped near the entrance to the pony-cart ring and walk toward him. She had a Village look about her that made him think of Julie, but she was taller and more slender and she wore her hair, which was a light brown and not flamboyant like Julie's red, in neatly plaited squaw braids. "You're Timmy Hale's father, I'll bet," the woman said to Frank in what struck him as an extravagantly droll voice. "You have the same ears. I'm Tina Hamilton's mother, Charlotte." Frank had heard of Tina, who was in Timmy's class at City and Country. He thought her mother attractive, and though he could find little to say to her it didn't seem to matter. They walked with the children through the Zoo and up the stairs past the bear cages into the Park. Already Frank had discovered that Tina had a crush on Timmy and they both had a crush on horses, that Charlotte had been divorced since Tina was a year old, and that Charlotte knew Julie from mothers' meetings at the school. They wandered through the Park, circling the skating rink, and came to the high ground overlooking Central Park South, where there are massive outcroppings of granite and many trees. The day was warm and bright. While Tina and Timmy climbed on the rocks, Frank and Charlotte sat in the sun. He had begun to talk now and found himself telling her about his work at the Foundation. "I gave away four hundred thousand dollars last week," he said. "Can you believe it? And I have forty-two dollars in the bank." He laughed, thinking that was the wrong thing to say. Charlotte laughed. She took off the white windbreaker she was wearing and held it in her lap. She had on a tank top, striped blue and green, and a blue denim skirt, and sandals. Her arms and legs were still dark brown from the summer, and the bleached down seemed to catch and hold the light of the sun. Her graceful and extravagant gestures made Frank conscious first of her body and then of his own. He felt pleasantly stirred. All at once she rose, letting the windbreaker fall to the ground, cried "God, look at this *day!*" and stretched her arms above her head. Frank got to his feet, picking up her jacket. Above their heads was the low limb of a sycamore; standing on tiptoe, Charlotte grasped it and, arching her back, let her arms take her weight. A wood nymph, Frank thought. An Indian girl, with those long braids and wide-set brown eyes. He had the sharp, surprising sense that he belonged just where he was—that they both belonged there—and that he had always been there, holding that white windbreaker, with this woman before him, both of them one with the dappled bark of the sycamore and the yellowing leaves on its branches and the luminous blue of the late afternoon sky. Looking at her, he was suddenly overcome by desire, much as he had been ten years before when Julie, wearing a lime-green summer dress, had walked across the room to him through a Village party crowd, fixed her eyes upon his, and asked him his name.

Frank telephoned Charlotte the next day after work to ask her out. Some day the following week would be about right, he thought, if she would see him at all. Why should so attractive a woman be free? "I wondered," he began. "I wondered if you would like to have dinner—"

"Tonight?" Charlotte said.

Hearing her voice made Frank say yes, tonight would be fine.

"I didn't think you'd call," Charlotte said. "I'd heard you were shy." It was too late for her to get her babysitter. Why didn't he come over there?

Tina met Frank at the door and hugged him about the legs. As he had always done with Timmy, he picked her up and kissed her. On her way to bed later, she turned toward him and said over her shoulder, "Will you be my daddy?"

Charlotte laughed. "Pay no attention to her," she said. "She's a ham."

Frank did not sleep with Charlotte that evening, but he did the next week when they saw each other again, and by November they were seeing each other nearly every night. "You do sweep a girl off her feet," Charlotte said. "Not that I mind." In early December, although he was not yet able to bring up divorce terms with Julie, Frank and Charlotte had begun to talk about getting married.

On the weekend before and the weekend after Christmas, Frank took Timmy to visit Charlotte at her parents' home in Connecticut, a few miles from Ridgefield. Tina, who was more sociable than Timmy, liked to invent games. One night at the dinner table she said, "All those with a bad habit raise their right hands!" Frank, who felt uncomfortable making love to Charlotte under the family roof, looked sidelong at her. Charlotte smiled and raised her hand. Frank raised his. He looked then at Charlotte's mother, who had raised her hand and sat smiling benignly at them both. She *knew* they were sleeping together, he was certain, and she was giving them her blessing. He lowered his hand. She *wanted* Charlotte to marry him. The whole family did, even her father. Why? It wasn't for his money, God knows—but *they* had that. Was Charlotte unmarriageable? She didn't look it. But then why had she been divorced so young, and why was she still unmarried? It was beginning to look to him like a family conspiracy.

But Frank did not ask himself too many questions. Pleased to be making love with pleasure again, and with someone who wasn't Julie, and pleased to be treated so warmly, he went along, watching the tide of his infatuation with Charlotte curiously at first—he had not expected to fall in love again so soon —and then giving in to it. Perhaps he *could* reach the center again, after all. And how lovely Charlotte was! How undemanding! How light her touch! None of Julie's heavy explanations. None of Julie's reasonings. In fact, there was little reasonable about Charlotte at all. His head was filled with her; she had nearly put Julie out of his mind.

Charlotte was a coquette, but what did it matter? She knew it and made a joke of it. She loved to tell him of her conquests and of the flirt she once was. She had run off to Hollywood and been a photographer's model for a while, and had yelled "Buddy!" at what she thought was an old chum in a Beverly Hills parking lot and Marlon Brando had leaned out of a window and yelled back and taken her to lunch. And at a resort in Arizona when she was fifteen she had been practically propositioned on the dance floor by a Justice of the United States Supreme Court; he wanted to go horseback riding with her, he *said*. And there was the party at the end of her senior year in college when everyone was drunk on sherry and she had got cream puff all over her face and her professor of comparative religion had come up and licked it off, slowly, slowly, and told her she was a goddess. And one summer on Majorca when she was eighteen everybody on the beach kept thinking she was Ava Gardner. What a summer that was!

Frank found her vanity charming. She was forever braiding or unbraiding her hair, or putting in her contact lenses or taking them out, or doing her nails or her eyes. Timmy and Tina played like brother and sister. Charlotte's father was in *Who's Who*. He was rich. Charlotte's family was small. Julie's family was poor, and there were so many of them! Charlotte had expensive things and simple tastes. Charlotte didn't mind washing dishes, and Julie, who had been made to wash them since she was five, did. He was happy. He had been really happy once before, the year after he graduated from college, when he lived near Florence one spring with a complaisant Australian girl, and he saw Charlotte in that benevolent Tuscan light. White walls and narrow archways. The *Maggio Musicale*. Strolling the Lungarno hand in hand. Espaliered trees. Botticelli. The high laughter of nuns in a cloister garden. On those weekends outside Ridgefield, Charlotte would come into his bedroom when the house had grown quiet for the night, wearing a translucent blue nightgown, her hands crossed lightly over her breasts . . .

. . . in thin array, after a pleasant guise,
When her loose gown from her shoulders did fall,
And she me caught in her arms long and small . . .

It is no dream; I lie broad waking, Frank would think. Had he ever been quite so content? They would make love to each other silently in the great house. I am giving her strength and calm, he thought. She is restoring me, and I will give her my strength.

Frank began to take Timmy every week again, and on Saturdays and Sundays in January he and Charlotte, with Tina and Timmy, began apartment-hunting in the Village. One afternoon after a heavy snow they walked through the West Village down the middle of the quiet streets, admiring the old red and brown houses with their frosted porticoes and window frames. In Grove Court they all lay down and made angels in the snow. Charlotte wanted to live in one of the old houses in Grove Court or Macdougal Alley or Washington Mews. But they were the most expensive parts of the Village. Wasn't that out of the question? Where would they find the money? Frank mentioned this to Charlotte and she laughed. Her father would help them, she said. But I can't take *charity,* Frank thought. Doesn't she know that?

Early in February, Frank took Charlotte to a dinner party given by the Watermans, a couple he and Julie had known through most of their marriage. "Would you like to hear what Doc Waterman said about your girl?" Julie said the next time he picked up Timmy.

"My girl?"

"If you want to be so secretive, why did you take her to Doc's house?" Julie said, and giggled. "Doc said it was nice to be able to turn your wife in on a new model."

"Charlotte's older," Frank said. "She's three years older than you."

"Doc said we're so much alike. We look alike and we talk alike."

"You don't," Frank said, realizing for the first time that they did. "Actually, you're poles apart."

Charlotte began to talk about marrying in the fall. She had got a Reno divorce, she told Frank, and there was nothing to it. Julie could take Timmy during the summer and do the same; it would be a nice vacation for them both. Then Frank and Charlotte could fly south for a honeymoon in Lima in the Peruvian spring. They would buy silver things and alpaca rugs from the Indians and sell them for heaps in New York and the trip wouldn't cost them a thing. They'd make money.

Could she be serious? Frank tried to reason with her. He had no savings, let alone capital—she knew that—and Julie took half of what he brought home. Where was he supposed to find the cash to buy the stuff in the first place, let alone pay their fare? All Charlotte would say was, "Don't *worry*." But Frank worried. Would her father pay for it all, then? Did they want her married that much? He was beginning to think they would do anything to get her off their hands. But he wouldn't take her father's money; he couldn't. They would have to live on what he had, and how was that possible? And how could he bring up divorce now with Julie? She was in no hurry, and God knows what her lawyer would do when they found out he was.

"I'm a butterfly," Charlotte had said to Frank the first night they slept together. He hadn't believed her then—but perhaps, after all, she was telling him the truth. At a party in March for her thirtieth birthday, to which she invited several old boy friends, Frank came upon her in an embrace with one of them —a light one, it is true, and in the living room; she was quite open about it. The sight humiliated and pained him more than anything of the sort since Julie had told him of her first lover, years before. What if Charlotte were not so different from Julie after all? Would she, too, have her infatuations, and would he once more have to find himself able to understand and to forgive? The thought that he was repeating himself filled him with dread. He could not go through all that again.

One evening Charlotte met another old boy friend, just in from the Coast, for drinks. It was only for an hour or so and Charlotte had asked Frank if it was all right, but he spent the time waiting for her in stubborn anguish. "Betrayed. Betrayed," pounded in his head, though he knew this could not be true. Then why was he thinking it? Did he *want* to be betrayed? Had he wanted Julie to betray him? Had he somehow been encouraging her to betray him all along, over and over again? Would he encourage Charlotte sooner or later? Was that what he was doing now by letting her have these drinks with this old beau? Should he have said no? How could he have been civilized and say no? These considerations disturbed him, but he thought he saw how extravagant they were and tried to put them out of his mind. He said nothing of any of it to Charlotte, who was home by half-past eight, a little high, but he found with chagrin that, as it had been with Julie during her adventures, their lovemaking that night was impassioned and free.

He had rarely been angry in his life, but an unfamiliar asperity over which he had little control began to seize him now and then. Once, in a crowded movie in the Village, Charlotte took a single empty seat and left him standing alone. The film bored him, the back of the theatre was hot and airless, and although he returned before long he left the theatre in a blind rage and had three drinks in a bar two blocks away before he began to be calm. He found Charlotte holding a seat for him when he got back. "I was thirsty," he said. He was unable to say more.

On another evening, while he and Charlotte were making

love in her bedroom, Tina awoke and began to cry. Charlotte left him and went to the child, who was a long time falling asleep, and Frank fell into a fit of jealous anger that he knew was infantile. But in anger a man can see the truth, he thought, and now he saw his situation as it was. Charlotte was a spoiled, vain, silly girl, and incapable of genuine love. There was no real feeling of love with her, no depth, no exchange. No wonder her father was ready to buy her a husband and caretaker! No wonder they thought him a good catch! What if he *was* poor? Money was no problem to them. They had seen him be patient and forbearing and kind. Well, he had been patient and forbearing and kind with Julie, too. . . .

He rose from Charlotte's bed and dressed, but he could not bring himself to leave the apartment, and as he paced the living-room floor his anger melted away. His passion for Charlotte was dying, he thought—yet he felt pity for her and for Tina still. He went back to the bedroom and undressed and got into bed again, but two weeks later, although he thought he cared more for Charlotte than before and more than he could remember ever caring for Julie, he left, announcing his departure as suddenly and formally as if he were proposing marriage. He put the blame upon himself. He was too unstable, he said. Perhaps it was too soon, and he hadn't gotten over Julie yet. Perhaps he wasn't ready for marriage.

"Ready for marriage?" Charlotte said. "You're not ready for divorce."

Perhaps he should be in therapy, Frank said, though he had no use for it; he didn't want himself explained away. Perhaps they both should be. Julie and Timmy were both seeing doctors now and it seemed to be doing them some good.

"You must hate me," Charlotte said quietly. "Why don't you yell at me or something? You're so reasonable all the time. You're so considerate. You're so God-damned polite."

And now Frank couldn't stop talking. He was *jealous,* if

she wanted to know what it really was, he said. And he *hated* it—hated the feeling, hated his weakness. She was too pretty. She had too many beaus. He loved her and he was jealous of her and he couldn't stand it. That was the real reason he left Julie, he said. He was jealous of her and he couldn't stand the constant pain. Surprised to hear himself say it, he thought that it was true.

Charlotte heard him out, then walked to the door of the apartment with him. In the hall, she waited with him for the elevator as she always did. They kissed goodbye. "Call me in a couple of days when you're feeling better," she said. As if, Frank thought, what he was suffering were no more than a touch of the flu. He exploded. "I'm *tired* of women," he cried. "I'm tired of courting them. I'm tired of being nice. I'm too *old* for courting. I'm sick and tired of asking, asking, asking and always being the asking one!" He heard himself shouting in the hall.

"You should go back to Julie, I think," Charlotte said.

But that was impossible, he thought in the elevator. Things had gone too far. He might love Julie still, he supposed he did, and he loved Timmy, but it was impossible. It would destroy him. She had given him too much pain.

"What you need, Frank, is a cow," Julie said when Frank told her he had broken off with Charlotte. "I mean that sincerely. Find yourself a plain, sensible girl. Get yourself several. Don't zero in so hard. You said you needed enough to touch you all around."

"You spoil us. That's your trouble," Julie said the next time Frank saw her.

"You're living beyond your emotional means," she said.

"Have you been talking to your therapist about me?" Frank said.

"What do you think we talk about?" Julie said. "By the way,

I have a new beau, but he's not really serious. For one thing, he doesn't have any money. Dr. Chisolm says while I'm in therapy I mustn't get too serious."

I am paying for Dr. Chisolm, Frank thought, and it will be a long time before she asks for a divorce.

Frank went with Lolly Parker, who worked in the Foundation's public relations office, to a free concert of madrigals in the Great Hall of Cooper Union. Lolly had known Charlotte when they were both working in fashion. "I went with her for a while," Frank said. "We were sort of engaged."

Lolly looked at him understandingly. "Charlotte was always 'sort of engaged,'" she said. "Charlotte never quite connects. She's a little mad."

Of course she is, Frank thought, and how he missed her! How his body missed her. Julie was a little mad, too. Could he only love women who were pretty and mad?

Determined not to drop out of circulation as he had after he left his wife, Frank began to date the receptionists and typists and secretaries and researchers at the Foundation. They were pleasant girls, a year or two out of college, most of them. They had quick minds and intended to make something useful out of their lives, and they were, as one of them said to him, highly over-qualified for their jobs. Frank found to his surprise that plain as most of them were he enjoyed making love to them, and at first he took a kind of intellectual pleasure in observing the similarities and differences in their bodies and in their sexual predilections. His self-esteem fed on his conquests and his appetites increased. But they were hardly conquests. Most girls went to bed with him willingly, and he did not think it was merely because he was conventionally good-looking, though he was. It seemed a matter of principle with them not to deny themselves new experience. He never stayed with one girl for long, and he was usually seeing two or three. He began to keep a diary, and at the end of each month he tallied his score. The notion of promiscuity in itself excited him, and it occurred to him now and then that perhaps he was trying to put himself in Julie's place. He was beginning to see what she saw in it, at any rate, but with none of her nonsense about first having to be in love. No one talked much about love.

He was more masterful now, he thought, and as the months passed his lovemaking grew harsher and more impersonal. Often, a girl would not rouse him enough, and he would have to summon up images of other women; fleshy creatures were the most effective, he found, in old-fashioned calendar-art poses. But the pictures he saw at the last—when he had finally succeeded in pushing himself to orgasm, the girl by this time usually lying spent beneath him—rose without being called. They were images of Julie or Charlotte in attitudes of abasement and surrender.

But although these girls might ask nothing at the start and never talk of love, soon each would begin to ask or give too much, and Frank's desire would flag entirely. He asked nothing of *them;* he would give them nothing. And they were all so *innocent!* How he missed Charlotte's deftness sometimes, and her indifferent air. One girl got out of his bed in the morning, when he had not wanted her to stay the night, and began to clean his kitchen, singing. Another brought him a glass of orange juice, freshly squeezed, while he slept; waking, he found it on her bedside table. Then she sat on the bed and fed him— *fed* him!—chicken livers and scrambled eggs. A third, a temporary file clerk, took him to her room after they had had three martinis after work. Martinis made her cry, she said. She told him that she had a seven-year-old boy somewhere in upstate New York that she hadn't seen since he was six months old. Would Frank help her find him? She had lost his address. He would try, Frank promised, for he had not seen Timmy in three weeks and he was moved by remorse, and the woman gave herself to him, weeping. But the next day he found he could not bear the sight of her, or bear the burden she had placed on him.

He did nothing to find the child and he did not take the woman out again. For the two weeks she was in the office, he would not meet her eyes.

By the fall, at about the time Charlotte had planned for their Peruvian honeymoon, Frank acknowledged to himself that she had never left his mind. She had a hold on him and the others didn't. She had forced nothing on him, really, in spite of her harebrained plans, and the others had, or had tried to. Julie had, he saw now; she had intimidated him for years. He could no longer stand seeing his wife or talking to her, and because seeing Timmy meant seeing her, he rarely saw Timmy. But Charlotte! She asked for little but what he could give, and the others seemed to *need* so much. And then he had betrayed her by leaving with almost no cause. Alone or in bed with a girl, he would wake now and then and find that Charlotte, or someone that might have been Charlotte, was in his dream. He would be searching for her through the rooms of an enormous Japanese hotel; was she a prostitute there? Or he would read in a copy of the *Daily News,* some weeks old, that she had been found dying in a Harlem tenement, then seek through the cemeteries of Queens for her in vain. After that dream, shaken by longing and fear, he called Charlotte and they had drinks one afternoon after work. She was friendly. They talked about Tina and Timmy and their families and their jobs, much in the way he and Julie used to do. Then Charlotte excused herself to make a phone call. She was engaged now, she said, and she had promised her fiancé she would check in.

It quickly became clear to Frank that whatever he felt for Charlotte was no longer love. The bodies of more than a dozen girls, his easy conquests, lay between them. He had joined the company of her old beaus. He watched Charlotte walk across the room toward the phone booths. She was putting on weight.

She was no longer his. Her chatter bored him. He felt neither jealousy nor desire. With a clear conscience, he gave her up.

He gave up the girls at the office, too, for flashier creatures that he met during the autumn at parties and in bars—women who had "been through the whole bit," as one of them said and as Frank was beginning to feel he had himself by now. But how much *more* they had been through! And how innocent he was of life still. How calm and gentle, in comparison, his life with Julie had been. There was one woman, an actress who looked twenty-seven and was thirty-eight, who had run away from her husband the month before. They had been living in a Boston hotel during the run of a play. Her husband was insanely jealous and beat her—not for anything in particular, she said, just for what he imagined—and each night he locked her clothes in a closet so she couldn't get away. For months she stole change from his pockets a little at a time and cashed it in for bills that she hid in the lining of her dressing gown. One night she hid his false teeth—he was much too vain to appear in public without them, she said—and ran away, wearing his trench coat over her dressing gown and his *zoris* on her feet. Frank believed her. On her buttocks and back and thighs he saw the green bruises. But why had she *hidden* his teeth, he thought. Why hadn't she hated him enough to throw them away?

Another, no more than twenty, Frank met in a bar in the Village. She was hungry and he bought her a bowl of soup. That was all she could eat. She had had an abortion the week before and hemorrhaged after, alone in her apartment—a sixth-floor walkup without a phone—unable to move. An old boy friend who still happened to have a key had come by, she said, or she would have died. She drew away when Frank first touched her. "You could say my life has been one long trauma," she said. Frank spent the night holding her, in her bed, the mattress stained with her blood, thinking that she was someone it was possible to love, not as he had loved Julie and Charlotte, but in the way he had loved when he was a child. And at the same time he was certain that he would not see her again. She was studying modern dance. She had modelled for detective magazines and showed him stills of herself in attitudes that made him remember his erotic images of Julie and Charlotte. In all of them, whatever the situation, she wore the same black brassiere, panties, garter belt, and stockings. She was now very, very thin, and her body and the body in the photographs were not the same. There were other photographs, too, taken of her on the tarpaper roof of her building. She was wearing a leotard and her body was bent into various artistic poses. "Look at this one," she would say. "This is closer to what's really me."

With a third woman, married and only recently separated, Frank moved congenially through drinks to her sofa and toward her bed. As he lay down beside her she said to him, "It's only fair to tell you, I guess. I tried to kill myself with gas last week."

Was she lying, asking for sympathy, Frank wondered. No one used gas anymore, did they? His desire for her increased. "I want you," he said, and caressed her. But the woman began to tremble. He tried to enter her and could not. "It's no use," she said. "I can't. I want to so much but I can't." She laughed. "I still love my husband," she said.

"It's all right," Frank said, as he began to stroke her and console her. "It's all right. I know how you feel. I've been through it too."

Later that night, having found the woman inconsolable and having drunk several bourbons alone in his apartment, Frank, too, began to tremble. He lay down on his bed, curled up with his knees close to his chest, and shuddered in long, convulsive tremors that had their source in his abdomen and groin, continued for several seconds, rippling out to his extremities, ceased, and then began again, over and over, before they subsided and came to an end. They were not unpleasant, but they frightened him. I am entering the circles of the lost and the damned, he thought—but this was Dostoyevsky's world and not his own. Until the last year his life had been placid enough. Why was this happening to *him?* What had he done? He supposed an outsider might see the long months since he had left Julie and Timmy as a deserved punishment, and he supposed the fates or God might be punishing him for leaving them, for abandoning his son, for being irresponsible, for wanting to be free. His relatives, he supposed—Julie's relatives, certainly—thought these things. But what else could he have done? He couldn't go on with Julie. He had done nothing without justification. He had not been cruel—unless letting Timmy down was cruel. Was suffering and a life without love all he had to look forward to now, at thirty-two? He couldn't believe it. He had loved Julie and he had loved Charlotte and he had suffered, loving them, but never in this loveless, hopeless, hollow way. He knew enough people to touch him all around, God knows—women, anyway—and now it was the touching that gave him pain. Just that—as if their flesh were burning. Though what was *his* pain, even now, compared with the suffering of that woman tonight, or the girl hemorrhaging alone in her room, or the woman covered with bruises? And there was nothing he could do for them. They asked for kindness—what else had those girls from the office been asking for?—and being kind for more than a moment to someone he did not love exhausted him. Then must he go back to living alone? No, that was impossible. His need for a woman was too great. Should he go back to Julie? No, that was impossible, too.

When Julie called the following week to say that she was going to marry Dr. Chisolm and wanted a divorce and full custody of Timmy, Frank was only faintly surprised. He agreed, though he was a little shocked at how indifferent he now felt toward Timmy, and how easy it was for him to let his son go.

The following month the lawyers drew up the papers, and after he and Julie met in her lawyer's office to sign them, Frank bought her a cup of coffee at a Schrafft's nearby. He was on edge. They were both on edge.

"I hear you've been going out with young chicks," Julie said.

"That was some time ago," Frank said. "You would have been proud of me. I had a new one every week. I was a monster. I seduced them and abandoned them."

"You always were sort of a monster, Frank," Julie said. "Dr. Chisolm says that's what you did to me."

"What kind of lies were you telling him?" Frank said. "That wasn't what happened at all. I've been reading my Bible. We loved each other and we were one flesh, and that lasted for a while. But you became a fornicator and I put you away. Matthew 19 something something."

Julie's eyes grew wet. "You zeroed in on me," she said. "I really only loved *you* from the time I met you." She looked at him earnestly. "You got to me first," she said. "All the others were only parts of you."

"But that's *crazy*," Frank cried. "What made you think you could run a marriage that way forever?"

"I would have stopped," Julie said. "Dr. Chisolm says I would. All you had to do was tell me. You failed to assert your masculine rôle."

Frank got up. "That's a lot of crap," he said. "Wow. Poor Dr. Chisolm. What a lot of self-indulgent crap! You were a bitch, don't you know that? For years there you were a spoiled, self-righteous bitch." But his voice was gentle. He had never used the word to her before, he thought. It was what men called women in anger. He put his hand on her shoulder. "You're a very pretty bitch," he said.

"You're the one who left," Julie said. "Just remember that when you're old and gray."

Frank went home and got drunk. Oh God, he thought. It was probably true, and Julie had loved only him. But had *he* ever loved anyone else? Could he ever? Weren't all the others, if you loved them at all, no more than reflections and echoes of the first one? Yet it wasn't even Julie he had loved so much as what she reminded him of. Not his mother—or not only his mother. It wasn't that simple. It went deeper than that. There was some figure of the Female—of that terrifying but sustaining power, not a man's own, which promises to make him complete—lying beneath *all* the images, beckoning to him through them, through Julie and Charlotte, through them all. Just as the Male beckoned Julie and the rest. The phallic god. Especially Julie. And the madder, the less domesticated a woman was, the closer she was to the Female. And the more desirable she was to him. Which is probably why he stayed with Julie as long as he did, and wanted her more when she was wild than when she wasn't. If it hadn't been for the jealousy and the pain. . . . And in spite of all of it, he wanted Julie still. And to get away from the circles of the damned.

Was it possible that marriage—even marriage to Julie, with all its pain and mess—offered the only way to get out of going around in circles, around and around? With the adultery and all, so long as there was passion? Just as long as there was that. Forget jealousy. Forget convention. Forget that Biblical crap about one flesh. Let Male and Female join, no matter how or where! Images of the women he had made love to appeared before him, and images of Julie with her lovers. We are *all* one flesh, he thought. We are all one flesh. He was too drunk to sustain the idea, but for a moment he felt it flow through him and release him like a revelation.

But it was, of course, much too late. In the morning he knew it was too late and was far from calling Julie and suggesting a reconciliation. What little he remembered of his thoughts the night before made no sense. On the whole, he considered himself lucky to get out of the whole business as gracefully as he had, and with as little pain.

And so Frank and Julie were divorced, and Julie married Dr. Chisolm and they moved to Washington, and time passed, and Frank's life began once more to be reasonably serene. He was head of a department at the Foundation now, and had enough money to rent a garden apartment in a brownstone in the East Eighties. Once in a while, Julie would be in town for a day or two and call to suggest that they get together, but they never did. Frank tried to visit Timmy, in Washington, at least twice a year. The boy resembled his mother strongly, and had some of his stepfather's mannerisms. He called Frank "Daddy" still; he once forgot himself, though, when Frank was there, and called Dr. Chisolm "Dad." It occurred to Frank less and less often to think of himself as a father, or of Timmy as his son. Summers, he would go on long vacations alone, to England or Italy or Greece. For nearly two years he had a pleasant arrangement with his secretary, and occasionally he would see one of his old girls again, but nothing went deep. For the first time in his life, he felt reasonably self-contained and free.

The girl Frank fell in love with finally did not look at all like Julie or Charlotte. She was blonde and slender, her family had never been very poor or very rich, she didn't talk much, she wasn't terribly vain, and she was affectionate in ingenuous ways that Frank liked. She would take his arm while they were walking or ruffle the hair on the back of his neck when they were alone, and she would wake him sometimes in the morning by tracing his eyebrows with a finger or tickling his ear. Frank had the uneasy feeling that all this, at his age—he was now thirty-seven—was more than he deserved. Yet although the girl was younger than Frank and had never been married, she was not, after all, so very young—she was past twenty-five—and he liked her not being ready to sleep with him until they had known each other for a time. He felt his passion for her to be strong and unswerving, as hers was for him, and he could not believe that they would ever cause each other pain. They did not talk much about themselves at first, but in a Second Avenue bar near his apartment one night, when they had both felt securely in love for quite a while, the revelations, half joking and half in earnest, began.

"I've been different since I met you," the girl said. "I'm usually not like this. I used to be quite mad. I freaked out all the time. I was capable of practically anything."

"Don't give it a thought," Frank said. "I'm a bad risk myself. I went through a lot in my day."

"I met a guy on the street on my lunch hour who had a real thing for me once," the girl said. "It was ridiculous. He was going to Chipp's to buy a sports jacket and he made me come along. I couldn't shake him. He always trusted my taste, he said. Then he had to buy me a drink."

Frank felt a jealous twinge and fought it down. "Other women have considered me a monster," he said. "Watch out. They say I abandoned them."

"*You?* A monster? You must be kidding," the girl said. "You're the most attentive man I've ever met. I've grown quite dependent on you. Not that I mind."

"What if I take you over?" Frank said. "What if I move in on you until all you can think of is me?"

"You're funny," the girl said. "What's wrong with that? I *need* that. I never felt closer to anyone in my life. I love you."

"What if the day comes when you feel smothered? What if you start wanting other men? What if you feel they're parts of me?"

"What are you talking about? You *are* funny."

"I'm not funny," Frank said. "What if that's how it will be?"

"Oh, Frank, don't be ridiculous," the girl said. "Come on. Let's go to your place. Let's go to bed."

Late Show

While his girl friend, Nancy Weaver, in wrinkled black Bermudas and a black sleeveless blouse, goes through her two bedroom closets weeding out her clothes, Peter Shaw lies heavy on her king-size bed watching the Late Show, an old Dietrich movie. Nancy has been meaning to get at her closets since early spring, when she and Peter met, and now it is late September. She has too many clothes, so many that there is no room in her closets for anything new. Some things have to be thrown away. And if they marry (Nancy has said to herself) Peter will move in; her apartment is twice the size of Peter's and less expensive. If that happens, he will need a closet of his own. Peter, in the T-shirt and chinos he wears around Nancy's apartment—they hang in her hall closet when he's not there—is propped up by a mound of throw pillows covered in bright cotton prints, orange and gold and purple and pink. His hair is bleached yellow, his skin still dark from weekends with Nancy on Fire Island. He was thirty-four in August, and though he is in good shape after the summer, the flesh accumulating about his waist and the deep lines that lead from his broad nose to the corners of his mouth suggest the ways in which his body will age. Beside him on the white nubbed-cotton bedspread are the clothes Nancy has already thrown away; they are to be given to Alice, her three-day-a-week maid, who may keep some of them.

The rest Alice will send down to West Virginia, where her sisters still live and where she has a daughter about to be married. On the floor at the foot of the bed is a tangle of wire hangers and crumpled pink and white tissue paper and another pile of clothes, a smaller one, to be sent to the cleaner's in the morning. Before Peter on the television screen, framed between his bare feet, Marlene Dietrich and Gary Cooper are having dinner with John Halliday. Halliday draws a gun. Gary Cooper kicks the dining table and the gun flies out of Halliday's hand into a serving dish. Cooper calls a servant. "Pedro," he says, "take the plate to the kitchen and disarm the fricassee." Peter and Nancy laugh. There are lines in the movie that delight them both.

The bedroom is hot. For the past few days the thermometer has been in the eighties, and Peter and Nancy have gone back to their summer drink, gin and tonic, drinking slowly all evening, tasting the last of summer. They both like the heat and the easy life it enforces upon them. Since seven, when Peter came over from his studio, they've been drinking and watching television, eating whatever was around the house—liverwurst and sweet-pickle sandwiches, Fritos, hard-boiled eggs, cold chicken. Stephen, Nancy's four-year-old son—she has been divorced for two years and Peter for five—watched with them for a while, but he seemed to be getting a cold and at eight Nancy put him to bed. After the late news she suddenly decided to do her closets, and now it is nearly one.

This is the first time since her divorce that Nancy has gone through her clothes. When she was married she traveled a lot with her husband—to Vera Cruz and Acapulco, to Miami Beach, to the Costa Brava, to Paris and the Italian Riviera—and was unhappy in most of those places most of the time. The dresses in her closets remind her of her unhappiness. She has worn few of them since, but many of them are good things and she has not been quite ready to throw them away. Now, with Peter, she is. And there are the clothes, some of them sheer folly, that she has bought since the divorce, when she would go on mad shopping sprees, buying things she might wear once or not at all.

Peter should be at the studio working tonight—he is a freelance photographer, in the middle of a job due the end of the week—but he can be only vaguely uneasy about it. The night is just too hot, and when Nancy asked him to keep her company while she did the closets he could not say no. He is her Marc Antony, and Nancy his Cleopatra; he knows it. She keeps him from his work, his career; he is bound to her by silken fetters he cannot break. She is so beautiful, in a strange, animal way— like a fox, like a pet fox. She is more beautiful than his first wife, more beautiful than any of the models and actresses he's had for girls. He is almost certain that he loves her and that he will marry her. But isn't it too soon? Divorce, which has impoverished him, has made Nancy almost well-to-do. If they marry now, before his wife remarries and he is free of paying alimony, Nancy will lose her alimony and they will both be poor. There is good reason for delay.

Nancy lives in an old, solid apartment building on Washington Square, in the place her husband had at the time of their marriage. It is rent-controlled still, a fabulous bargain. Her bedroom is huge, and everything in it but the furniture is painted a deep yellow-gold—the walls, the ceiling, the woodwork, the doors, the light switches, the window frames, the shutters that cover the windows and bar the view of a brick-walled court. Nancy painted the room herself after her divorce. The furniture is white—a white wicker chaise longue with purple cushions, white chests, white marble-topped tables on each side of the bed. The carpet is gold. On the wall facing the bed in a white rococo frame is a large oil portrait of Nancy when she was nine, in a maroon velvet dress.

Nancy is still dark brown from their weekends in the sun, and the gold room, Peter thinks, becomes her. She has been working rapidly, but now and then she will stop to hold a dress up to herself and examine her appearance in the full-length mirror, still spattered here and there with flecks of yellow-gold paint, that is set in one of the closet doors. Sometimes, standing before the mirror and posing for Peter, she will ask his opinion of a dress. His opinions are brief; his eyes are on the movie.

Now, on the screen, Gary Cooper is dealing with the man who had the gun. In the mirror Peter can see Nancy's reflection. She is looking at him by way of the mirror, holding up to her shoulders a lime-green sleeveless dress. "Do you still like this one, Peter?" she asks. "Should I keep it?" Between Peter and the reflection is Nancy, her back toward him, barefoot, in black shorts and blouse. Her hands, holding the dress up to her shoulders, make him think of the tabs on a paper doll dress. "Peter, tell me what you honestly think of it," Nancy says.

"It's a nice one. It looks great," Peter says.

"But I wore it so much this summer," Nancy says. "And last summer I wore it to death." Peter, thinking of Nancy before he knew her and of the times she must have worn it during what she calls her "promiscuous period," says, "Then throw it away."

"I'll keep it," Nancy says decisively, and hangs it back in the closet. "I'm terrible if I like a thing."

For a time, clothes fly. Quickly, holding one thing after another up to herself for Peter to see, Nancy throws away:

- a yellow plaid sundress, *much* too long, with spaghetti straps, one broken
- a black crepe dress, straight up and down, with a straight band of black satin down the front
- a white ribbed cotton coat with a flare skirt and a large, flat bow ("I really like bows. Too bad," Nancy says.)
- a pair of hip huggers, brand new, black, a size too small
- a fitted black cotton sheath, six years old
- a pair of white pants, man-tailored, with grass stains on the seat and a triangular tear in one knee

Nancy was a Powers model for a while before she married. Now she clowns for Peter, giving him a mock fashion show of the ragged and out of date.

"My God," Nancy says. "It's like throwing your *life* away."

Their glasses are empty, and Peter goes out to the kitchen to fill them with ice and tonic and gin. "I'm stoned," he says when he returns, and he lies back upon the pillows with one knee bent, pressing the bottom of the cold glass against his forehead. Except for the thin voices from the television set and the rustle of tissue paper and dresses, the room is quiet. Peter, breathing lightly in the hot air, looks at Nancy through half-open eyes. How lovely she is, he thinks. . . . But will he ever really touch her? "Come, sit down for a while," he says. They watch the end of the movie together.

On the television screen, Marlene Dietrich and Gary Cooper stand before an official at a table. Marlene Dietrich wears a light coat with a high blue-fox collar. "Look, Nancy," says Peter. "They're getting married."

"My God," says Nancy. "How I'd like to be married in *that*."

The loud music as the movie ends wakes Stephen in the next room and he cries. He is thirsty and feverish. Nancy goes in to sit beside him on his bed while he falls asleep and comes back to find Peter watching the Late Late Show, an Abbott and Costello comedy. Peter has turned the volume all the way down for Stephen's sake, and because he likes to watch old comedies without the sound. They are funnier to him that way. Sometimes he and Nancy will guess at the plot and the lines; sometimes, like tonight, Peter will simply look at the images on the screen, mindlessly.

Now that it is still, noises from the other apartments on the courtyard come through the window—mutterings from other television sets, a dog whimpering, the closing of a refrigerator door. And then there is a woman crying, saying over and over, "I can't. I can't. I can't." Peter shuts the window and turns on the air conditioner. It, too, is painted gold. The machine shudders, gathers force, and settles into a soft, liquid roar. It is old, from the first year of Nancy's marriage. "You know I never have it on," Nancy says. "We'll be breathing straight dust."

In a few minutes the bedroom becomes cooler and closer, and fills with the smells of old houses, unbeaten rugs, bicycle oil, vacuum-cleaner bags. Half-hypnotized by the flickering images on the screen, Peter watches Nancy moving at the edge of his vision. Nancy, absorbed in work, forgets him. She has come to dresses she hasn't worn for years and years; memories of old times assail her. She is almost thirty now, and settling down. Tonight she feels that she has begun to leave her youth behind —and with how little pain, it seems, how little regret!

How beautiful she is, lost in her own world, Peter thinks again. How beautiful! How far away! That is how she will always be, he thinks. I will never quite reach her. And yet how happy I am just watching her. If only, he thinks, I could hold on to this moment, lying on her bed and watching her. If only I could hold it forever in the palm of my hand. . . . He drifts, half asleep, and an image, more fragile than memory, floats into his mind. He is lying on his mother's bed, too young or too ill to move, and his mother, wearing a burnt-orange dress and jet beads, bends over him. He sees the pale round of her forehead, the protecting curve of her shoulders, the cleft between her breasts. This is where I have always been happiest, he thinks—in a woman's bedroom, on a bed that is not my own. I am sinking into this bed, he says to himself. I am sinking. I shall drown in perfume and dust. Remembered beds, remembered girls float before him. What if Nancy is no more than that— another image, another bed? Peter shivers. I will soon be thirty-five, he thinks, and what have I done? I will be thirty-five and

I have done nothing and tonight I cannot even rise from this bed. He begins to lift himself up on his elbows. "I should go back," he says.

"Wait a while," says Nancy. "I'm nearly through."

Peter waits, while the pile of clothes on the bed grows higher, so high now that he can see nothing of Nancy but her head and shoulders. "How extravagant she is!" he says to himself. "Look at her—throwing a thousand dollars' worth of clothes away!" His stomach knots. He remembers the truth— that he will never have enough money to marry her. He can never afford her and he will have to leave her. The prospect is a stone upon his chest. He has had women he couldn't afford before and he has left them. He catches his breath, taking in air that is cold and heavy with dust, and remembers dank places— cisterns, vaults, open wells, the cellar at home in St. Louis smelling of vinegar and coal. When he was a child, he would wake shivering from a nightmare of frogs swarming out of the toilet bowl in his grandmother's house. The sudden memory of it chills him and he sneezes, so hard that he sits upright.

"God bless you," Nancy says. "It's the dust."

Peter sneezes again and lies back among the pillows. "I'm catching Stephen's cold," he says. Nancy turns off the air-conditioner and opens the window. Now she is wearing a long black velvet theater cloak, so long that its hem touches the floor. She models it for Peter, holding it open to display its pink satin lining, then lets it slip off her shoulders to the floor.

She picks it up and drops it on the bed. "Out it goes," she says. "I've had it eight years and I've worn it exactly twice." She sits down beside Peter, lights a cigarette, and looks thoughtfully at the pile of discarded coats and dresses. Most of them are black. "I used to like black," she says. "After Bill and I were separated, that was all I wanted to wear."

"It's sexier," Peter says, sitting up and blowing his nose.

"It wasn't that. I had the feeling nobody would see me if I wore black. I could walk alone into P.J.'s or any place and go unnoticed. Black made me feel invisible."

"Did it work?"

"No. I never had so many propositions in my life. Including most of my husband's friends. And I didn't want to see anyone. Not at first."

"I know," Peter says. He takes a cigarette from Nancy's pack and lights it. "It's the worst time. After Louise and I separated I *didn't* see anybody. I moved into a cold-water flat on East Seventh Street—Louise was still living on East Tenth then—and I did it over. It was a fifth floor walk-up with a view of the moon and the Empire State Building and it cost twenty-two forty-five a month. I painted the floors glossy black and the walls dead white. I painted the undersides of the sink and the tub in the kitchen black. I hung red burlap curtains on the windows. I had a flush door on saw horses for a work table and a flush door for a bed, with a foam rubber mattress covered in red sailcloth that slid off on to the floor whenever you made love. I took a couple of dressers and tables from Louise and painted *them* black. I bought black chinos and a black sports coat with red stripes and I sat there in a black sling chair reading *Le Rouge et Le Noir*. No kidding. Somebody told me it was *the* guidebook to success. I wanted to make it, like Julien Sorel. But I couldn't concentrate. After three weeks I was looking for women."

"All that red and black must have been bad for your nerves."

"It wasn't just me. That was the style. I lived my life in flats and lofts that looked like botched Franz Klines. My days were a waste of black ink and white paper—I had a job then laying out a trade weekly—and my nights were a waste of black-and-white movies and girls with white faces and dark-shadowed eyes, and cafeterias, and coffee houses, and bars stinking of beer, and wet black streets at four in the morning."

"I always have liked color," Nancy says, considering. "There was just that time with the black dresses, and one winter I wore black tights a lot."

"It was all too bleak to live with for long," Peter said. "Finally, the color began to come back. After a few months I moved in with a girl on Commerce Street who had blue walls and white woodwork and yellow straw rugs. Framed Swedish travel posters. Pâpier maché Mexican roosters. Twelve mirrors. Butterflies under glass. Magic-lantern slides. I lay around there all summer while she cooked dishes out of old *Vogues* in her yellow Belgian pots and we played Orff and Vivaldi on her hi-fi."

"What happened?" says Nancy, getting up to go back to her closets. "Go on. I'm listening."

"She had spells. She brooded on Sundays—she couldn't help it—and she used to throw me out on Sunday nights. I was still so demoralized at that point that I'd call her on Mondays and come right back. I would sit in her bathtub looking at the skin shrivel on my hands and tell myself I had to get out, I had to get out. Then I went to Nantucket alone for two weeks in September and made up my mind to leave, but when I got back, all ready to tell her, she had a fever of a hundred and two. Virus pneumonia. I stayed with her through that for two and a half weeks, and when her temperature had been normal for twenty-four hours, I left. 'No wonder you've been so goddam nice to me,' was all she said."

"Was she worth it?"

"Everything's *worth* it, one way or another."

Nancy sits down beside Peter again. "With me, it was different," she says. "At first, after Bill and I were separated, I didn't go out at all. I sat at home and went to pieces, eating tuna fish out of cans and the stuff Stephen left—pureéd lamb and prunes. Now, when I break up with somebody, I make myself go out again right away. It's like getting back on the horse. I start out by giving a party."

"Every time I used to break up with a girl, I'd move and fix up a new place," Peter says. "Not any more. I haven't got it in me."

"I'm tired of it," Nancy says. "I don't want to go through it again. I'm too old. I'm tired of telling guys about the time I impaled my lip on a fence spike the year I was eight, which accounts for the cute little scar, and why I won't eat cheese. I'm tired of being sexy and charming, and the whole routine. I want to settle down. You don't *know* how I want to settle down. I'm almost thirty."

"I'm tired, too," Peter says. "Hell, I'm thirty-four. I've been at it longer than you."

"Excuse me," Nancy says, getting up once more. "I've *got* to finish these clothes."

"You *like* to throw things away, don't you?" Peter says.

"I don't. I hate it. My God, you should see some of the things I've kept." Nancy hesitates, standing before the closet door. "I kept the suit I was married in," she says. "I wasn't going to tell you. The thing's hopeless. Padded shoulders. Fitted waist. It's a good suit, though. Black linen. I bought it in London and I paid eighty guineas for it. It *must* be unlucky to throw away your wedding dress. I couldn't."

The enormity of Nancy's extravagance, set against his own poverty, suddenly overcomes Peter. "Look at you!" he cries out to her. "Look at these piles of *clothes!* Is that *all* you care about —CLOTHES?"

"Sh-h-h," Nancy says. "You'll wake up Stephen."

Peter rises to his elbows, whispering. "How can I afford you? *You* know how much I make and how much I pay Louise. I've leveled with you. You know what I can afford right now."

"Nothing?"

"That's exactly right."

"You can afford me if you really want me," Nancy says, as if she were indifferent. "I'm adjustable." She stands, looking down at him, and goes on, analytically and without anger. "I think you like being broke," she says. "I think you're proud of it. You like being in the situations it keeps you in. You *like* being helpless. You like to lie here and know that you can't support me and you've said so and I love you anyway. And you like to be moral about the way I spend my money. Why shouldn't I spend my money any way I like?"

"It's Bill's money, isn't it?"

"You don't have to *argue* with me. This isn't an argument. It's a problem, that's all. Look at *you*. You know what you throw away? Time. You've thrown away more years of it than I have and there's no way to get it back. Don't talk about *my* extravagance. You know what *you* are? You're extravagantly *poor*. Don't turn on *me*."

"I'm not turning on you," Peter says wanly. "But how can I afford you?"

"Think about it."

Peter begins to get up off the bed. "I'd better go back," he says. "I'm stoned. I can't talk about it now."

"Don't go—not yet," Nancy says. "I don't want you to *leave*. Just think about it."

"What the hell do you think I think about? It's an impossible situation."

"Do you love me?"

"Oh, for God's sake," Peter says. "Yes."

"Then what's all the fuss? I told you I'm adjustable."

"You're so extravagant," Peter says, and sinks down on the pillows.

"All right," says Nancy. "I'll have to reform."

"This is the last one," Nancy says. "I want you to see it before I give it away." She has changed into a fussy red organdie party dress with a puffed-out skirt and cummerbund waist. "This was my cotton-candy dress," she says. "I wore it at the party Bill and I gave when we first got back to New York, when we invited forty and ninety-five came."

"Turn around," Peter says. Nancy turns, then pirouettes before him. The back of the dress is cut very low. The dress is too tight. Peter can see a fold of flesh pinched under Nancy's arm.

"It's too young for me," Nancy says, standing flatfooted before the mirror, inspecting herself. "I can't wear full skirts any more." There are tears in her eyes.

"Right now you look exactly eighteen," Peter says.

"Oh God, I know. I know I do. It's maddening. Can't I start looking my age?"

"Why? Why change? I don't plan to change until I'm fifty."

Nancy is still looking at her reflection. "When I do get old," she says, "it will be all at once, like Margo in Shangri-La."

"She had *left* Shangri-La," says Peter. "That was her mistake. She fell in love and left and then she withered away. Who knows? Someday we may really fall in love and grow old like everybody else."

"I love this dress," Nancy says. She turns toward Peter, and her eyes are full of tears. She lies down beside him, tucking the full skirts under her, and gives him her hand. "I never thought I would have to grow old," she says. "I didn't think I'd reach thirty. I'm not *ready*."

"People never are," Peter says, and turns to stroke the hair back from her temple, knowing it soothes her. He has seen her like this before. She lies still with her eyes nearly shut and begins to talk, slowly. As if I were her analyst, Peter thinks.

"The year I was twelve, after Father died and Mother and I began traveling," she says, "Mother took me to a fortune teller in Santa Monica. Not a gypsy or anything. Just an unpleasant woman in a flowered housecoat who read my palm and told me I would have three unhappy marriages and die young. Can you imagine living with that when you're twelve? I *believed* her."

"You've only been married once."

"I've had two unhappy affairs that were just as bad. And I *should* be dead. She was right. I was almost killed once. Haven't I told you about the time I was almost killed?"

"Tell me."

"I need a nightcap," Nancy says. Peter gets up and comes back with two more drinks. Nancy has taken off the red party dress, which sits on top of the pile of clothes, and lies on the bed in her blue robe.

"It was on my honeymoon with Bill," she says. "Are you sure you want to hear about it?"

"Sure."

Nancy lies flat upon the bed. Peter cannot tell whether she is being melodramatic or not. "After Bill and I were married in London," she says, "we bought a Jag and drove through France into Spain on our honeymoon. That was when people were just starting to go to Spain. We were driving through the Pyrenees in late October. It was cold and there was a little snow. Bill was asleep and I was driving, late in the afternoon. I came into a curve too fast, that was all. The road was icy and I lost control of the car. There was a sheer drop and no barrier. It was a lousy road. I couldn't bring the car back. It wouldn't respond. I knew we were going over and there was nothing I could do, so I took my hands off the wheel and waited."

"Were you frightened?"

"Are you kidding? I was terrified. I'd been expecting something like that to happen for years, but not on my *honeymoon*, for Christ's sake. I was *happy* then. I loved Bill. I was only nineteen. I thought about waking him but then I thought, why should I ? Let him go in peace. There was nothing anyone could do. So I just sat there and waited and then the car took the curve and came on back. I just *sat* there and the car came back. I drove down to the next town and then I woke Bill up and told him he could drive."

"You're a good driver," Peter says, stroking her hair.

"It wasn't me. That's the point. It wasn't anything I *did*." Nancy sits up and looks at Peter. "Something stronger brought us back," she says. "I could feel it. Just as if a hand had moved us back on the road. I was being saved. It was a funny feeling, like suddenly feeling loved. I *know* I was being saved. But what was I being saved *for*?"

"Stephen?" Peter says. "Me?"

"Oh, I don't know. I don't know," Nancy says. "All I ask out of life is a sudden quiet death."

"Hush," Peter says. "Don't."

"My father had cancer of the blood and it took him six years to die. I couldn't bear it."

Nancy is weeping. "You were young when he died," Peter says.

"I was *eleven*. I was old enough to be nice to him and I wasn't. I couldn't stand watching him die. I wouldn't go see him."

"Don't think about it," Peter says.

"It's not painful any more. I worked it out with the analyst years ago. It just took him such a long time."

"How old was he when he died?" Peter asks.

"Forty-nine. They say forty-nine is the hard year for men. If you can get past that, you're safe."

"*Safe?*"

Nancy almost giggles. "Safe for a while," she says. "Safe through your fifties." She blows her nose.

"I want to be safe for longer," Peter says. "I want to live to the twenty-first century."

"What for? You'll be past seventy."

"I want to say I've seen it. I always have."

"Is *that* what you've been saving yourself for? My God," Nancy says. "Is that what you've been doing? Sparing yourself so you'll *last* longer?"

"It wasn't that," Peter says seriously. "I've never had much of a sense of urgency. It's the way I was brought up. My mother gave me too much love, I think. I believed I had all the time in the world."

"Nobody has *that* much time," Nancy says.

"Oh, I feel the urgency now," Peter says. "When I came here from St. Louis I gave myself ten years to make it in New York. I've got three years to go."

"You're going to have a busy three years," Nancy says.

"I'll make it."

"Are you sure you want me around?"

"Sure I'm sure," Peter says. He sits up, crossing his legs like a tailor, and faces Nancy. "I need you. You're good for me," he says.

"I don't know," Nancy says. "Maybe I'm bad for you. I'm vain, frivolous, superficial, and extravagant. You've said so yourself. My doctor says I'm a luxury. 'Do you intend to be a luxury all your life?' he says."

"You're good for me," Peter says. "I need incentive. I need to be pushed. I want to take care of you. I want to buy you things."

"I like you to buy me things," Nancy says, and puts a hand on his arm. "But it's not important. Not really." She pauses. "There's something else I wanted to tell you," she says, and begins to speak more slowly, looking down at the bed, her voice thick with remembered feeling. "When I was first married to Bill, before things began to erode," she says, "I was very much in love. We had a reception after the wedding and there was a minute when Bill and I sat in a corner talking and people left us alone. I was so happy. I knew I could tell him anything and he could tell me, and we didn't have to say very much if we didn't want to because if we wanted to we could say anything. I knew we were going to be happy, and it was such fun."

"Yes."

"I haven't had that feeling with anyone else and I have it with you. I can talk to you. We have such *fun*. I don't want to lose that again."

Peter lies down and draws Nancy to him. "Let's get married, Peter," Nancy says. "Let's get married soon."

We are moving too fast, Peter thinks. We are beginning to move too fast. And he kisses her, opening her robe, his hand upon her breast.

The door to the bedroom creaks and Stephen walks in. He wears no pants, only a faded knit pajama top, and he moves stiffly, like a child who has just learned to walk. "I dreamed about you, Mommy," he says, and stares at the television set. "That's Bud and Lou," he says. "What're you watching *them* for?"

Peter and Nancy sit up, and Stephen looks at them. "Were you kissing?" he says.

"We were hugging," says Peter. "Besides, it's very late." He gets up and begins to move Nancy's clothes from the bed to the chaise longue in the corner of the room. Nancy takes Stephen and holds him to her. "He's burning up," she says.

Peter feels his forehead.

"Don't touch me," Stephen says.

"It's nothing," says Nancy. "It's his tonsils. It happens all the time. We're trying to keep them until he's seven."

"I'm hungry," Stephen says.

Peter goes to the kitchen and brings Stephen a dish of ice cream. Nancy moves the rest of the clothes from the bed, and Stephen sits next to Peter, eating and watching Bud and Lou. He falls asleep finally, leaning against Peter, breathing heavily. Soon Peter eases him down upon the bed. "Don't touch me," Stephen says, and is asleep again.

"Would you carry him?" Nancy says, and Peter lifts Stephen up in his arms. Carrying the child into his bedroom, Peter feels awkward, and as if he were playing a part. Nancy is Stephen's mother, he says to himself, and at this moment, when he is full of desire for her, he finds this difficult to understand. But if we marry, he thinks, I will become his father in time, and he will be my son. Is that possible? Stephen is burning, and Peter drops him upon the bed, his head at the foot, as if he were too painful a burden to bear farther. Stephen whimpers but does not wake, and Nancy turns him around and draws the covers up over him.

"God, Nancy, I'm dead," says Peter as they leave Stephen's room. "I'd better go."

"No, stay," Nancy says.

Peter takes off his T-shirt and his chinos and his shorts and drops them on the chaise longue, on the pile of Nancy's clothes. Forgetting to turn off the television set, he tosses the colored pillows from the bed to the floor, pulls back the bedspread, and eases his way between the flowered sheets. In a moment Nancy, naked too, joins him. They embrace, and quickly and silently, in the fitful light from the television screen, they begin to make love.

"Tell me a story," Nancy says later, her head in the crook of his arm, and Peter, remembering the frogs of his early nightmare, tells her of a frog transformed into a prince. She drops off, and before long, having settled into the bed and turned on his side and locked a pillow in his arms, he begins to follow her. We are getting older, he thinks. I can't leave things up in the air much longer. I've got to make up my mind. . . . But soon sleep bends over him, and Peter, drawing the pillow to his breast, slowly submits to her. Before his eyes a red sports car, high in the mountains, slews around a curve out of control and comes back, as if moved by an invisible hand. Something will happen soon, he thinks. Something will happen soon, and then I can decide.

Take It Easy, Edna

"No girls in *this* band," Augie Leonard said. "Girls in a band are trouble." We were sitting, I remember, at the counter of the Mona Lisa Ice Cream Shop, a shady rendezvous not far from school. I could barely understand him. He was sucking on a chunk of cracked ice, and some record—"Song of India" or "Sometimes I'm Happy," I suppose—was thumping from the jukebox behind us.

"Not Edna Kohler," I said. "She's no trouble. Wait'll you meet her." Our band had no piano, Edna played the piano, and at this point she seemed to me our last hope. Augie, who had transferred to our high school that year from Saginaw, farther upstate, had persuaded a number of us to form a dance band—a purely private enterprise, for this was in the fall of 1937, some time before dance bands became part of the official high-school music curriculum. Augie had played trumpet for a couple of years around Saginaw with a group called the Fiery Five, and now he wanted a band at least twice as big. This, he had told us, would be a good year for big bands, both sweet and swing.

So far, we had recruited nine men from the high-school marching band: two trumpets (including Augie), a trombone (me), two alto and two tenor saxes, a bass fiddle (who played sousaphone in the school band), and a drummer who doubled as vocalist. Augie planned to lead our band from his seat in the brass section. But we couldn't locate a piano player, and without one our rhythm was weak and the band didn't hold together. None of those we had heard were right. Either they played only by ear, or they had no ear, or they were good enough to want pay for rehearsal time, which was out of the question. Or they were girls.

I had proposed Edna before in jest. I was proposing her now in desperation. We had come from another desolate session in the basement of the Unitarian Church—where we had just been asked to find another place to rehearse—and the empty thunk and swish of bass and drums, uneasily trying to fill in the hole where a piano should have been, was still in our ears. Without somebody to play the piano, we were cooked. "All right, what *about* Edna Kohler?" Augie said, and fished out another chunk of ice from his Coke.

I didn't know much about her, except that she played the piano—classical music—and had been playing as long as I could remember. Her only outside interest, her only "activity," was the piano. Under her picture in the high-school annual— she had graduated the previous spring—there was nothing but "Talent Assembly, 1929-37" and *"Still waters run deep."* She had taken part in the Talent Assembly, an annual benefit for the school book fund, every year since she was in the fifth grade, and by this time she had become a town tradition and a town joke. Each year it was the same. They'd wheel the grand piano out on the stage, one of the boys would walk back again to get the bench, and someone would cry from the audience, "Here she comes!" And out Edna would come, wearing a new dress, frilly and modest, of rose or light-blue taffeta, and with her hair in a fresh permanent. She would stand at the piano facing us, bow a jerky little bow, and tell us, in a thin voice, that she would play for us this étude of Chopin's or that sonata of Scarlatti's, some piece of music that we had never heard. Once she had seated herself and begun to play, we were more comfortable. Until then, it was all most of us could do to keep from laughing.

"What was so darned funny?" Augie asked me after I had described Edna's public performances. I couldn't tell him, really. We saw her every day, and she was so plain and ordinary, and then there she would be up on the stage, once a year, trying to look like a performer. She was so *dedicated,* and she took it all so seriously, and the contrast between the once-a-year Edna and the school-day Edna was just too great. But she wasn't really funny, I said to Augie finally, she was sort of sad.

She could play the piano, though, I was sure of that, and she wouldn't be any trouble in the band. None of the guys would be fighting over *her.* Not that she was ugly or peculiar. She was plain—a pale blond German girl from the other side of Michigan Street who hadn't yet lost her baby fat, with straight, thin yellow hair that she kept trying, hopelessly, to curl. Her father was Ed Kohler, the butcher, and her friends, if she had any, must all be from the German part of town. No one I knew knew her any better than I did. She hadn't gone on to college; she was working in the Sears, Roebuck store downtown. She usually wore cotton dresses that looked homemade and low-heeled shoes.

"Low heels," Augie said. I think that may have convinced him that Edna would be harmless. No girl in low heels could break up a band. Our girls, the girls around the Mona Lisa that year—Peggy and Clara and Jean and Red, the girls who would drink whiskey-and-Coke and play hearts with us—wore sweaters, knotted kerchiefs, tweed skirts, Tweed, and heels that were high for that time. They could be trouble; we liked them, but we wouldn't have them around the band. "Let's go talk to Edna," Augie said.

I thought it would be better to talk to her father first. Ed Kohler, who had a pork store on Michigan Street that had been started by his father in the eighteen-eighties, was about the most approachable man in the town. He was bustling and charitable, active in the Legion and the Lions, in on every kind of civic affair. He liked to encourage enterprise in the young, and had always been an easy touch for tickets to the school plays and concerts, or advertisements in the yearbook. Everyone in the school band knew him, certainly, for he sat next to us at football and basketball games, off at one side in the front row. Now and then lifted to his feet by some pounding march, he would stand before us beating out the time and humming, swaying like a captive balloon in a light breeze. His features were massive and noble, a little larger than life-size, as if he were wearing a heroic mask. He weighed perhaps two hundred and fifty pounds, which he carried with grace and, most of the time, good humor. People called him Tiny and laughed along with him. They were sorry, I think, that his one daughter had turned out so plain and shy.

We saw Mr. Kohler in his shop that afternoon, with Augie, who was a lot more persuasive than I could have been, doing most of the talking. Augie had a wide-open face, a nose twisted slightly askew, and the habit of underlining what he said with short, abrupt nods. Like his style on the trumpet—what we then called a mean horn—Augie was forthright and throaty, with a limited range. He spoke of the band the way my Scoutmaster used to speak of the troop.

"We expect a lot of hard work at first, Mr. Kohler," I heard him saying, "but we'll have some fun, and I figure we ought to do pretty well. This will be a good year for big bands. Full orchestration, lots of style, plenty of brass, everybody singing crazy words back of the vocal, like 'Marie.' That's what people want. I figure we can get all the jobs we can handle. Fraternity dances up the hill, the school, things at the country club. . . ."

"Some of the lodges, maybe," Mr. Kohler said.

"Sure, some of the lodges. Maybe the firemen's ball."

We already had most of the band, I said. Nine pieces—it was going to be a small big band—but we had to have someone really good on piano. Would Edna . . . ?

"We thought we'd talk to you first, Mr. Kohler," Augie said.

He stood behind the counter, listening to us, nodding, saying little. Then he asked us a few questions. Where would we rehearse? We weren't quite sure. How many nights a week would we rehearse? Two, maybe three. How much would the band make? Thirty-five, maybe fifty a night. He would talk to Edna about it that night, he said. He couldn't be sure. Of course, he said, we would want to hear her play first. Of course, we said. "Maybe it's a good idea," he said finally. "Maybe she doesn't have enough to do."

Two or three days later, he called me to ask us over to his house the following Sunday afternoon. Edna hadn't made up her mind, he said, but she would play for us. Then maybe we could decide.

It took Augie and me quite a while to find the Kohler house on Sunday. They lived in a lace-curtain neighborhood in the old part of town, where the lots were narrow and the two-story gray frame houses were set close together. Edna came to the door—I had somehow expected her father—and I introduced Augie. She looked nicer than I thought she would, though no prettier. She still had some summer tan, and her hair, bleached by the sun, was longer and gathered at the nape of her neck.

We went into the living room, where there was a baby-grand piano near the front window. Augie and I sat down on a sofa upholstered in faded green mohair. Edna sat opposite us in the matching chair. "I wanted to talk to you for a minute before Father came down," she began. She spoke hurriedly, with the echo of a German cadence and accent. "Of course, you were both very nice to want me to play with you, to play in your band. Father has told me all about it, and he thought I should play for you today, and we should talk, and then we would *see*. If you knew Father, you'd know what that means."

I was puzzled. "We just wanted to talk it over with you, Edna," I said.

She turned a little toward me. "How could you think I would be right for you? My training is classical, you know that. I can't play dance music. I don't mean to sound like a snob. I only mean I don't think I could play your music if I tried."

Augie leaned forward, elbows on his knees. "It's the same notes, Miss Kohler," he said. "Just less of them. If you can play Liszt, or Bach—"

Edna went on as if she hadn't heard. "I really don't think it would be wise, and my teacher thinks it would be most unwise, but my father . . ." She looked at me again. "You should have come to me first, you know," she said.

"Well, Augie and I thought—"

"I know what you thought. You thought you could get to me through him. But I'd love to play for you, anything you wish." She rose and went over to the piano.

She played for an hour or so, one piece after another, stormily at first but with more calm as time went on. Shortly after she began her father tiptoed in, greeted us silently, and sat down. Whenever Edna paused, Mr. Kohler would say "Very good" or "That was very good this time, Edna," and we would echo him. I was still embarrassed by Edna's chiding, so I was probably not a fair judge, but it seemed to me that everything she played sounded a little the same—too polished, too regular. Yet by the time she was through there was no question in our minds. We wanted her in the band.

We asked her finally to run through some popular music for us, but before she began, Mrs. Kohler came in—as plain as her daughter—and we stopped to have coffee and kuchen and talk about what a wonderful pianist Edna was. Edna said little; she seemed unmoved by praise. Then she took some sheet music out of the piano bench and played "Smoke Gets in Your Eyes," "My Man," and "Let Me Call You Sweetheart." She was note-perfect again, but somehow she made the tunes resemble each other. "Your left hand is very solid," Augie said. "That's good." Then we asked her to read off at sight a few of the piano parts from the band's arrangements. She stumbled a little at first, but in less than an hour, while Mr. Kohler moved about the room like a nervous pigeon, she caught on and began turning them out note for note—"Sweet Leilani" or "Sophisticated Lady," it didn't matter to her. I saw Augie's shoulders stiffen when Edna went through "Sweet Leilani" with the precision of a brass band playing a Goldman march. "She's as steady as a clock," he said to me. "That's what we need."

She had a lot to learn, but once or twice when Augie, who played the piano after a fashion, sat down next to her and worked over a phrasing with her, Edna picked it right up. It was becoming clear that, after all, she wanted to play with us. "What do you mean, you can't play this music?" Augie said to her. "Who do you think you're kidding?"

"But you'll have to be patient with me," she said to Augie, smiling a little, and that was that.

"You should hear her play 'Ist das nicht ein Schnitzel-bank,'" Mr. Kohler said.

"Oh, Father, stop clowning," Edna said.

There were details to go over. No pay, of course, until the band began to get work, and then, like the rest of us, an even share of what we took in. Edna would pick things up fine— she had a good sense of rhythm and a good ear—once she'd rehearsed a few times with the band. When, by the way, we found a place to rehearse, we said. Right now we hadn't any. Mr. Kohler was standing next to the piano, pulling thoughtfully on his right ear lobe. He paused, hand in air, as if he were standing at his block with his cleaver raised, about to cut a joint. The cleaver fell. "You can rehearse right here," he said. Augie and I made a few demurring sounds, but we were quickly persuaded. We agreed to assemble the band in the Kohlers' living room twice a week, starting Tuesday night. Edna and her father and mother saw us to the door, and we shook hands all around.

On the way home Augie and I stopped off at the Mona Lisa, still dazed, to have a Coke and listen to a few records. In one afternoon, we had acquired a pianist, a place to rehearse, and—although we didn't yet know it—an impresario, Mr. Kohler himself, our Hurok, our Diaghilev.

All that fall we rehearsed, two or three times a week, in the Kohler living room. It wasn't easy to fit us in. Bill Simmons, our drummer and vocalist, was squeezed with his traps in front of the window, next to Edna. The trumpets were on the davenport, I was on the matching chair with my trombone, the saxes sat on dining-room chairs, two in the living room and two in the dining room just behind. The bass player had to stand in the front hall, though his string bass was in the room with us. We neither felt nor sounded like the band we had hoped to be, but at least we could run through the numbers.

We had, by then, quite a lot of numbers to go through. Each of us had contributed three dollars toward building a music library, and Mr. Kohler had added ten of his own. Augie and I had driven in to Detroit and come back with an armload of arrangements, which then cost fifty or seventy-five cents each— standards, and current hits, and specials adapted from Goodman's, or Ellington's, or Tommy Dorsey's big records. All of us except Edna knew the records and would try to copy the solos on them—Harry James' trumpet on "Sing, Sing, Sing," say, or Dorsey's trombone on "I'm Gettin' Sentimental Over You."

By the end of November we were fully equipped. We had a name—the "Rhythm Rogues." We had music stands, painted black, with an "RR" monogram and a brace of eighth notes stencilled on the front. We had white Palm Beach jackets, maroon bow ties, and dark trousers, and Edna had a new white gown. We had our standards arranged in sets. Our "sweet" set, for example, included "Sweet Sue," "Sweet Georgia Brown," and "Ida! Sweet as Apple Cider!" Our "blue" set had "My Blue Heaven," "The Blue Room," and "Blue Skies." We planned to move from there directly into our "moon" set—"Blue Moon," "Carolina Moon," and "Moon Over Miami." And we had worked up several novelty numbers. In our version of "The Merry-Go-Round Broke Down," for instance, we all sang the chorus in unison while the brass and sax sections, alternately, did knee bends, for a carrousel effect.

Musically, however, we were not so good. We had been wrong, apparently, about Edna's picking things up. She read well and she seldom lost her place, as the rest of us did, but she seemed to have no sense of phrasing or jazz rhythm. She made her way through a piece as if she were all alone in the room, playing a Czerny exercise. She would give each dotted eighth and each sixteenth note precisely its proper value, for instance, and no one could make her understand that in dance music this was *wrong*. Nothing any of us did or said seemed to help much, though after a time the easier pieces, the waltzes and the ballads, were just about bearable. Edna was quite unprepared for being so bad. She knew she was a better musician than we, and she had been trained to habits of perfection. While *we* had been slouching in a classroom or sitting around the Mona Lisa, Edna had been practicing, practicing. I'm sure that to her ears no improvement in her playing was possible. Yet she knew something was wrong, and the harder she tried to set it right, the worse it seemed to be.

"The beat!" Augie would cry, thumping the floor with his right heel. "Where's the beat?" And Edna, trying to do it right, would fall on the second and fourth beats of each measure with a sandbag left, or pound through a chorus in the style we called

Mickey Mouse. "Take it easy, Edna, you're trying too hard," we would say.

"I'm *trying* to," she would cry, and slam her fists down on the black keys.

"Pick it up again at the chorus, fellows," Augie would say. "And, Edna, take it *easy*."

There were times when Augie and I took a good deal of abuse from the rest for picking Edna in the first place, and times when Augie would tell me it was all my fault, and I would reply in kind. At least once a week Edna would offer to quit, and we would all work at cheering her up. We couldn't let her go now. We were too deeply involved with her father and with her— and who else would we get on piano? Besides, there was something about Edna that we all liked. She was working so hard and so hopelessly and with such good humor to play music that, from her classical viewpoint, was hardly worth playing at all, and yet she kept trying. We all thought that next time, somehow, we'd get through to her. It became a kind of group project. If she'd only relax, we said.

Mr. Kohler, singularly deaf to our faults, was never far away, hovering over us, poking his head in every few minutes, now from the dining room, now from the front hall, coaxing us to take a break now and then when he sensed any strain. He knew we were having troubles, and his solution, from the first, was to get the band jobs. "Not yet, Mr. Kohler," Augie had to tell him again and again. "After the first of the year. We're still ragged." Then, shortly before Christmas, we were persuaded. First we played a holiday dance at one of the lodges Kohler belonged to, then another at the new junior high, and then on New Year's Eve we played at the country club, on two hours' notice, when the musicians they had hired from Detroit went off the highway into the snow.

We looked and sounded so much better on the stand than in the Kohlers' living room that for a time, in the holiday euphoria, we thought our troubles were over. They weren't. The Rhythm Rogues just didn't have rhythm. Even the ballads gave us trouble. Bill Simmons, as I have said, was both our drummer and our vocalist, and when he sang at the mike, in front of the band, he left his drums behind. He would begin to work his way up front a good sixteen bars before his cue, and this left the job of holding the tempo to the bass fiddle, who wasn't very loud, and Edna, who was. Then Edna, feeling the responsibility, would tense up and begin to race like an engine out of gear, and when Bill got back to his drums, just in time for the final chorus, nothing he could do would slow us down.

We had, at the very least, counted on Edna to hold the tempo steady. Alone, she was a metronome. With us, something went wrong and she lost control. "Take it *easy*, Edna," Bill would say as he edged past her, and we would whisper to her during the vocal, "Take it easy, Edna, nice and slow."

Not that we were much better than Edna was. But we had expected more from her. She was, after all, a musician. The rest of us were public-school instrumentalists, at home only in a few keys and in the lower and middle registers of our horns. We were happy enough to get through from start to finish without losing anyone on the way. I had the feeling most of the time that the music was playing us, and not the other way around. We would follow as best we could, and often lag a little behind. And all the time we were fumbling through a piece like "Blue Skies" or "Marie," we could hear in our heads, from the Goodman or Dorsey record, the way we *should* sound. It was a humbling experience.

In spite of all our failings, the Rhythm Rogues prospered. Augie had been right. This was a good year for big bands. Marginal producers though we were, we rode to prosperity on the soaring curve of demand. We were also the only bargain big band in that part of Michigan. Our price was usually no more than fifty dollars a night and sometimes less, and we split the money evenly among us. Mr. Kohler asked for nothing but the glory.

Mr. Kohler, though, did a great deal of the work, and we found ourselves more and more closely tied to him as time went on. We became his band, really. Not that he tried to take us over, not at all. But he found us most of our jobs, and he watched over us in other ways as well—jacking our price when he knew an organization was rich, seeing to our transportation if we played out of town. Mr. Kohler was, I suppose, the real reason for our success. No one could say no to him—at least, not the first time around. The dates he booked for us, plus a few fraternity and high-school dances that Augie and I found, kept the band busy nearly every Friday and Saturday night well into June. Mr. Kohler went with us almost always, driving his panel truck, with "E. KOHLER, PROVISIONS" in gold script letters on each side. Edna would sit next to him—she was seldom out of his sight—and we'd pile our instruments and stands in the back of the truck and follow behind in Augie's car and mine.

I would like to say that we improved over those months, but it wouldn't be true. All that happened was that we got used to ourselves and didn't try too hard—which was an improvement, in a way. People seemed to like us, especially the older crowds. I suppose they thought we were cute. Edna didn't change a great deal, though by spring we were able to kid around with her enough to keep her from tensing up too often and speeding the tempo. "Take it easy" by then would get a laugh from her, and for a while she would be all right. None of us ever talked to her much outside the line of duty. We had nothing in common, really, except the band.

I do remember an evening in late May, one of the rare times when Mr. Kohler couldn't come. It was a party for somebody's

silver wedding anniversary at the country club. The guests were
all drunk enough so that it didn't matter how we played, and we
were better than usual. I drove the Kohler truck and took Edna
home.

"I guess you must be glad the year's almost over," Edna said.

"Oh, I don't know," I said. "It's been a lot of fun." I could
just see her out of the corner of my eye, bouncing on the hard
seat next to me, her features lit dimly by the dashboard light.
She had changed since fall and seemed thinner, better-looking
in a way. The baby fat was gone. I could see the line of her
cheekbone now, and her mouth seemed more firmly set.

"You don't have to be nice to me," she said. "You've all
been too nice."

We were coming into town and I stopped for a light. "Well,
if you want to know," I told her. "I *am* glad it's over. A few more
weeks of this and I'd go out of my mind."

Edna giggled. "You know what it is? We're all just so *aw-ful*."

"I know it. I never heard anything so bad in my life." We
rattled down the hill toward the Kohler house.

"I know," Edna said. "And we couldn't get out of it. You
couldn't get out of it. I couldn't get out of it. Augie couldn't get
out of it—he's the *leader*. And heaven knows Father couldn't."

"He wouldn't. He thought we were good."

"I know."

"Why can't he leave us alone? He makes me feel like a slave
sometimes."

"I know."

"You can't help liking the guy," I said. "I just wish he'd
leave us alone."

"How do you think *I* feel?" Edna said. "It's been like that all
my life."

We decided to break up right after graduation. Edna, without telling anyone, had taken a job as a counselor in a music camp upstate. Augie had a summer job with the Fiery Five at a resort on Lake St. Clair, and I planned to loaf around the beach on Lake Michigan. We were scattering. There were no farewells to speak of, though the Kohlers had us all over to dinner the night before Edna left. Then Augie left, and I was getting ready to leave. And then Augie came back, bringing with him two of the original Fiery Five—Chester Freeman, piano, and Jimmy Williams, guitar. The resort job had fallen through, and they were looking for work. Almost at once it struck us that, except for Edna, the Rhythm Rogues were still around or could be brought back in. Chester Freeman would give us a good piano, and with the guitar we might have a solid rhythm section for a change. Perhaps then we wouldn't sound so bad. We decided to pull the band together again and look for a summer job. "We won't tell Kohler," Augie said. "Not until we find work."

We played that summer at the Crossroads Inn, a tavern just over the county line and twenty miles from town. There were eight of us—six from what we now referred to as the Original Rhythm Rogues, and our new piano and guitar. We worked there from nine to two four nights a week, Wednesday through Saturday, for five dollars each a night. The Inn was a squat corrugated-iron barn, hot and noisy and usually crowded. It was the nearest place to town where you could dance and have a few drinks, for our county was still dry. This was to be the Inn's last good summer, though. The county, after several tries, had gone wet in the spring election—repeal in Michigan was by local option—and the new law was to take effect on the first of September. The three hotels in town were already installing their bars.

The dances at the Inn were exuberant and sweaty, and we began to enjoy ourselves. Chester Freeman turned out to be a relaxed pianist, with sloppy technique but a lot of drive. His rhythm was strong enough to bring the rest of us to life. We began to jam a few standards, with Chester setting the key and tempo. Our "St. Louis Blues" went on and on for fifteen minutes or more, first slow, then fast, then slow again, under blue lights. We felt we were playing mean, dirty music; the crowd, most of them young and many of them from the small towns and farms nearby, loved it. Between sets we would go over to the bar for a beer and mingle with the customers. It was all so free and easy, and that summer I thought jazz was the only career.

One day Augie and I stopped in the store to tell Mr. Kohler what we had been doing. He was nice enough, and we were too young then to realize how hurt he must have been. It had all come up so suddenly, we said, and we figured he'd probably had enough of us anyway. We asked him to stop by and hear us sometime when he had the chance.

With Edna out of the band, we were quite sure Mr. Kohler would lose interest in us. At first, apparently, he did, but then he began to come by, usually on Wednesday nights when it was fairly quiet, and listen for a while. We kidded around with him, as we always had, but he seemed melancholy, like the old coach fired at the end of the season who's come back in the fall just to look the boys over. We began to feel sorry for him.

The Crossroads Inn had been doing so well the nights we played there that, early in August, we asked for more pay. We were turned down cold. The owner's position was simple: we could either go on as we were or quit. We went on, but when Mr. Kohler stopped by again a few days later with a brand-new idea, we were ready to listen.

What Mr. Kohler proposed, and we finally accepted, was that we set up our own dance hall at the county fair, which was scheduled to open at the fairgrounds just outside of town on Friday, August 26th, and to run through Labor Day, which was on September 5th. We would play every night, with weekend matinées, and all the profits would be ours. Except for recovering his expenses, Kohler wouldn't take a cent. He already had an option on the space, and a cousin in Detroit would lend him a tent for the cost of trucking it over and setting it up. We should take in, he estimated, at least a hundred and fifty to two hundred dollars a day. Less his expenses, that would leave us something near two thousand dollars to be divided among us. This was good money—half the amount would still be good. Even with Mr. Kohler and Edna back with us, it seemed worth it. Nothing had to be said about Edna; she had come back from camp the week before, and we all understood she was part of the deal. Chester Freeman, as soon as he saw what was going on, got sore and quit. So did Jimmy Williams. It was too speculative for them, they said.

The Rhythm Rogues closed at the Crossroads Inn on a Saturday and opened the following Friday at the county fair—seven of us now, including Edna. Mr. Kohler wanted to surprise us, and none of us had gone to look at the dance hall before our opening night. Augie and I picked up Edna at the Kohler house, since Mr. Kohler had been busy out at the grounds all day. Edna was in good spirits. She had made wonderful friends over the summer, she said, and she was going to music college in Chicago in the fall.

The dance hall, a tent that had been constructed for a Grosse Pointe lawn party the spring before, was beautiful. Circular, about thirty-five feet in diameter, it was pitched in a field just between the exhibition buildings and the entrance to the midway. The roof was red-and-white striped canvas, a blue pennon fluttered from the tip of the center pole, and wire screening covered the sides. Inside, the yellow center pole gleamed with spar varnish, and there were white-and-blue canvas camp chairs placed along the walls. The bandstand, off to one side, was raised above the dance floor; potted greenery was ranged across the front, and there was a white upright piano for Edna. A mirrored ball, high inside the tent, reflected coins of light upon the floor. Outside, above the entrance and suspended between two poles, rippled a spotlighted banner that read:

ED KOHLER
Presents
THE RHYTHM ROGUES
$1.00 PER COUPLE

"Good Lord!" Edna said.
"I didn't know about that," I said to Augie.
"Neither did I."
"Now we've got a sponsor."
"It's a beautiful tent," Edna said. "But I don't think anybody is going to come."

She was very nearly right. Something—none of us knew what—went wrong. Our music couldn't have been that bad. The first night, Friday, we played from seven to nine-twenty-five before anyone came in, and our total paid admissions that night were, as I remember, twenty-two. People came up and looked. They stood outside the screen and peered until we felt like performing apes in a wire cage, but they didn't come in. Well, we said, Friday night is opening night. Everyone would naturally be more interested in the livestock and the jams and jellies. "They're older than I expected," Mr. Kohler said, standing under his sign with his hands clasped behind his back, looking at the crowd. They were young enough for the midway, though; they shuffled past us toward the pitch games in a persistent stream.

The second day, Saturday, we had about fifty in the afternoon and a few more than fifty that night. "It's building up," Mr. Kohler said about nine in the evening, and for the first time since we had opened he sat down. Sunday was about the same, and then, from Monday through Thursday, there were never more than three couples on the floor at one time.

Poor Kohler. He began to wander about the fairgrounds, looking at the crowds in front of the exhibits and on the midway, puzzling over what had gone wrong. Now and then he would come back to look in on us—we found bitter pleasure in playing our engagement through to the end—but nothing we could say would cheer him. Like greater and lesser men before and after, Mr. Kohler had been carried away by blind pride and by love—for his daughter and, in a way, for all of us. He had hoped to build us a pleasure dome, but the county fairgrounds was not the place. Few people would come to the county fair to dance in a peppermint-striped pavilion—at least, not in 1938. Perhaps we were ahead of our time.

The disaster was so total that it became funny. By ninethirty Tuesday night, when we were well into our third straight hour of playing to an empty floor, we began to see how funny it was. Mr. Kohler had gone out for one of his thoughtful walks a few minutes earlier, and when he came back he brought a dog. He didn't mean to; the dog just came on in behind him. Augie spotted the creature first—a small, dusty terrier—just as Mr. Kohler sat down next to the ticket table near the entrance. "Hey, fellas—a *customer!*" Augie yelled. "A *dog!*" Bill Simmons began a drum roll, Mr. Kohler rose to his feet and looked around, Edna thundered on the lower keys of the piano, one of the trumpets blatted a ragged fanfare, and the poor beast yipped in fright. He couldn't find the way out, and skittered back and forth on the freshly waxed floor.

"Get him, Father, get him!" Edna cried. Mr. Kohler did. Weaving, slipping, falling once to his hands and knees, he finally herded the dog to the exit.

"Out! Get out!" we heard him cry. "Hound!" He came back in then, panting, his face flushed. "Done," he said heavily, and brushed the resin off his hands and then off his knees. We cheered. We shouldn't have, for Kohler sensed the derision in our voices. "Ach, I'm sick and tired of you fellows always horsing around," he said, then turned and left the tent.

But all we could do was laugh. "You know why he left?" Edna said to Augie. "He's going to collect admission from the dog." Augie began to giggle and found he couldn't stop, and that was enough to set the rest of us off into a fit of group hysteria that held us captive for what seemed half an hour. Then, just as Augie began to get a grip on us, Mr. Kohler came back. He could never stay sore for long. "How much did you charge him, Father?" Edna shrieked. "How much did you charge the dog?" This time, Kohler thought it was funny, too, or he caught our hysteria. He sat down in his chair and laughed with us until he cried.

For the rest of that evening, and for what remained of our stand at the fair, Edna and the Rhythm Rogues nearly played well together. It would be wrong to say that we began to swing, but we held the beat, and Edna even took a few choruses on her own.

Wednesday night, it rained. Augie and I brought a couple of girls from the old Mona Lisa crowd along, and so did one or two others. Mr. Kohler brought Mrs. Kohler. Taking turns off the bandstand, we danced with the girls, and with Edna, and with Mrs. Kohler. No one bothered us; the grounds were nearly empty. Mr. Kohler seemed in better spirits. Like many heavy men, he was a good dancer, and the girls made much of him. We all did. It was easy, for we were free of him by now. There was enough wind with the rain to dampen us inside the tent, and that night I caught a cold that grew during the week into a feverish grippe. But if the others could stick it out, I said to Edna, then I could, too. "The show must go on," she said, and giggled.

Thursday night I remember less clearly, except that my dreams after the dance were of empty ballroom floors in splintered moonlight, with the refrain of "Music, Maestro, Please," Kohler's favorite song, going around and around in my head. Friday and Saturday and Sunday are a blur. Sunday night after the dance, Mr. Kohler told us how much we had made and we divided the spoils. It came to ten dollars each, or not quite twenty cents an hour. Then Mr. Kohler made us another proposition.

"Tomorrow is the last night," he said, "and I thought it would be all right with you boys if we let the public in free. Sort of a Labor Day celebration and a last farewell from the band. That way we might get the crowd to come in for a while. I could even provide refreshments."

Mr. Kohler was pleading with us when he didn't have to, for we wanted to fill the hall as much as he did. By then we all saw, or felt, that it was really for Edna that he had done everything. He had hoped to surround her with young men, to build a summer palace for her and pack it to the walls. Now he wanted to make one last try.

"Sure, Mr. Kohler," Augie said. "Let's have a party."

Mrs. Kohler invited us all over for a picnic in their yard on Monday afternoon. Mr. Kohler wasn't there—last-minute things to do at the fairgrounds, she said. Around six, we drove out, Augie and I in his roadster, with Edna between us. The parking lot, to our surprise, was already two-thirds full. "I wonder what's in store for us *this* time," she said.

"Look at all the *cars*," Augie said.

There was a great deal of commotion in front of the tent, and as we worked our way through the crowd toward it we began to see why. "*Hon*estly," Edna said. "This time he's gone too far." There was a new sign. "FREE DANCING," it read, and below that, "FREE BEER." On each side of the path leading to the tent entrance there was a row of long tables, made of bare planks set on sawhorses. On the tables were ranged, at intervals of about seven feet, small kegs of beer. By each keg was a stack of paper cups. Behind each keg stood a man in shirtsleeves and white apron. Above the tables fluttered banners reading "HAPPY DAYS! RIVIERA'S HERE AGAIN!" A truck emblazoned with the Riviera emblem, a blatant yellow-red sunburst in a square blue sky, was drawn up by the side of the tent, and we could see more kegs of Riviera beer inside the open doors.

Mr. Kohler, as jolly as Santa Claus, stood near the entrance talking to a man who nearly matched him in weight and girth. This was Jack Brandell, he told us, of the Riviera Brewing Company in Detroit, with whom he had prepared our surprise. Mr. Brandell explained that he had been waiting since 1933 to introduce Riviera to our county, and when his old friend Tiny Kohler had called with this proposition he had jumped at the chance. No one had a license yet to sell beer in the fairgrounds, but we didn't need a license, because our beer was free. Kohler, the old fox, must have been planning this for more than a week.

We were being used, and we knew it, and we didn't mind. Brandell gave each of us a five-dollar bill, taught us the words of his company's jingle, set to the tune of "Happy Days Are Here Again," and then organized us into a marching band. We paraded through the fairgrounds, wearing paper party hats, with local youths behind us and before us holding signs saying RIVIERA BEER and HAPPY DAYS! We blatted out "Hail, Hail, the Gang's All Here" and "Happy Days Are Here Again" over and over, drunk by now with the idiocy of the entire enterprise. When we finally got back to the tent, the words of the jingle were dancing in my head. Every half hour or so, all evening long, we'd play "Happy Days" again and chant:

Riv-i-era beer is here,
It is the beer that
Brings good cheer,
So have a glass or two
Before you're through.
Riv-i-era beer is here!

Quite a few people had more than a glass or two before they were through, and our party turned into a happy bacchanal. The dance floor was filled for the first time—packed full—and the couples shuffled about through spilled beer, rustling the empty paper cups. Instead of closing at eleven, we closed at one, when the beer had all been drunk or spilled and most of the midway's booths and tents and rides had already been struck. Toward the end the carnival hands and barkers and pitchmen came around to hear. Mr. Kohler was never far away. We could see him standing off at one side of the floor, talking to friends, his white hulk polka-dotted with red and blue flecks of light from the reflector above. Then he would be swimming out of the haze toward us, to silence the band and shout another dedication into the microphone—this one, say, "To Clyde and Jennie Trumbull, of Twin Oaks, and their little girl Beverly, who's just turned sixteen." Then he would lead the band through "Music, Maestro, Please" once more, swaying before us, his great arms waving just a little off the beat. Then "Tiny! Over here, Tiny!" someone would yell, and he would be sucked back into the crowd, usually before we were through the first chorus. Everybody had a wonderful time.

During the last hour, Augie managed to pull us together and we played some of the numbers we had liked best ourselves. I remember Bill Simmons at the mike, standing sober above the crowd. "It's very clear," he sang, "our love is here to stay." His voice broke, and then he went on. "The radio *and* the telephone and the movies that we know may just be passing fancies and in time may go. . . ." It was a sentimental parting.

Mr. Kohler had his victory. I remember Edna best as we saw her late that night, after nearly everyone had left. She was being passed from one man to the next—most of them carnival hands —dancing, whirling, being kissed by them all. At last she was delivered to her father, who stood by the door. She was with him still when we broke away and headed for home.

Mr. Kohler was a little drunk. His wife stood on one side of him and Edna on the other, and he was hugging them both. "Have you ever seen anything like it in your life, boys?" he was shouting as we walked toward the parking lot. "Have you ever seen anything like it in your life?"

I Am Waiting

Nine o'clock—no, his wristwatch shows nearly a quarter after—and Ernest has been waiting for Maggie for three hours. If he knows her at all after practically living with her for two years, off and on, he has another two or three hours to go. Waiting for her is nothing new. He is used to it, really, though it still ties him up in knots. But tonight they were planning to eat out at a place in the East Sixties they only go to now and then when he feels flush, and Maggie said when they got up that morning that she would definitely be back on time. It is Friday and not one of the nights she often works late. (She's a fashion co-ordinator for TV and industrial shows and keeps impossible hours.) Ernest went straight to her apartment from his studio and got there a little after six, in time to put out the potato chips and make a clam dip and chill the double old-fashioned glasses they drink their martinis-on-the-rocks in before Maggie got home. (He's a freelance commercial artist and his hours are pretty much his own.) But Maggie didn't come home, and at half past seven he put what was left of the chips back in their bag, covered the clam dip and put it in the refrigerator, and made himself, finally, a martini. Ernest doesn't like to drink alone—it usually depresses him—but these long waits for Maggie give him a thirst. At eight or so, after a second martini, he went out to the counter restaurant a block away for a hamburger and french fries, knowing that when Maggie is this late she will not be back in time for dinner or want more than a bowl of soup when she comes in. On the way up to the apartment just now he bought two bunches of daisies at the flower stand on the corner. The flowers will be a distraction. When Maggie gets home, she will be angry—at whoever she's been with or at the cabdriver or at Ernest. Drinking after a point puts her in a rage. But when he gives her the flowers she will cry, "Oh, Ernest, they're *lovely!*" in her boozy, theatrical voice, and then she will go into the kitchen and arrange them, filling the Chinese bowl with ice water, carefully clipping the stems and stripping off the lower leaves. She loves flowers. Touching them calms her, no matter how much she has drunk. Afterward, she will want some soup, and after that Ernest can usually get her to bed.

The daisies are in the refrigerator now, and Ernest has settled down in the living room to wait, though he knows he will not be able to settle down. Why? Why is it? He knows that any evening may turn out like this with Maggie, and yet each time he thinks that this one may be different, and only when Maggie is an hour or an hour and a half or two hours late does he acknowledge to himself that once more she is out for a good share of the night. Now and then she will show up on time. "Surprise, surprise!" she will cry. "It's *me!*" But usually it is like this. He ought to know better, and yet again and again he will take her at her word, for again and again in the morning when they've just gotten up and are hung over and remorseful and sane she will give him her word and mean it. And he will be there early to make sure he can hand her a martini as she walks in the door. And then he will wait and he will grow anxious, though he knows better than to be anxious, and slowly, slowly, as it is now, his anxiety will rise.

Each time, too, he will wait as he is waiting tonight for the phone to ring, though Maggie rarely calls—only often enough for him to think it possible. Tonight, because they have not eaten a decent meal for days and were really looking forward to it this morning—to the baked fish in white sauce and the Chablis—he honestly thinks she may be working late and will call. But no one at all has called, which is strange, because usually people call on Fridays to see what's on for the weekend, or Maggie's mother calls from Darien. The phone hasn't rung once. Now Ernest picks it up to make sure there's a dial tone, and a few moments later, just to make certain the thing is working, he dials weather. It is the operator with a voice like Mae West's and he listens to the report three times. He is even more anxious than usual—almost ready, after hearing the recorded voice of that operator, to call someone, his father in Chicago or an old girl friend, just to hear a voice he knows. But what if he does and Maggie is trying to call him? What if she has tried already when he was on the phone? Though that's hardly likely. His nerves are getting the better of him, he thinks. He feels himself slipping out of control. He knows he's being neurotic, but where *is* she? Where in hell can she be?

But he knows where she is, even if he doesn't know *exactly* where. She's in a bar—a hotel bar, probably. By now, whoever she is with will be trying to get her out of the bar and into bed, and although Ernest knows she isn't likely to get into bed with anyone unless she is blind drunk, he also knows that once he lets himself imagine Maggie in bed with another man—once the picture of her copulating with another is in his mind—he will have no peace until she comes home. Oh, where is she? He doesn't mind the waiting, not really, only that it turns him into a jealous fool.

And it is only nine o'clock—well, by now it is half past—and he may have a good three hours to go. Time for him to take a firm grip. Time to turn on the tube. He flicks the channel selector, but there is nothing he can bear watching. He makes himself a drink, a Scotch this time. He feels safer on Scotch.

He can get away whenever he wants to, after all. Right now, if that's what he wants. All he has to do is go—he's done it before. And this time he will leave the keys to the apartment behind him. He's worked it all out in his mind. Then, if he and Maggie make up, he will not take the keys again, and when they go out he will call for Maggie at a reasonable hour—late enough to let her have her drink with someone, if that's what she wants. Eight-thirty or nine, say. A civilized hour. And then if she isn't there he can leave and that will be that. As it is, she *knows* he is waiting for her, and if someone says let's have one more—well, why not? She always *means* to make it just one drink after work, and it's knowing that Ernest is at home waiting for her that lets her stretch it to two, or three, or four drinks —by which time she's too far gone to care.

But he won't leave. Not tonight. How can he? They've been through too much together by now. He loves her. He knows she needs to be sure he is there waiting for her. And it was much worse at first. Then, before she had a job, in her unemployable days, she could go out in the afternoon for a drink, miss her date with him, and not turn up for a week. They are both more stable now. And she needs him. She has to know he will be there. Everyone else in her life has let her down. Her mother and father, and her husband, Nat, and the lovers she has had since Nat divorced her and took custody of the children. Besides, Ernest *has* tried to break away. They've split up five times in two years. But when they are together they *feel* things, at least sometimes, and separated they both go dead. Really dead. Into lives without life or resonance, into separate rooms with walls and floor and ceiling of cotton batting. Into cells. And then Maggie will phone or he will phone, and when he **hears her** voice—"Ernest? Is that you?"—he will run right back. Literally run. His studio is on the top floor of a tenement only four blocks away. If he ever intends to leave Maggie for good he will have to move to another part of the city and get an unlisted phone.

Once, Ernest thought there must be something he could really do for Maggie. There isn't. All he can do is make things easier for her, which is more than anyone else has been able to do. Her wounds go too deep. She exploits him, of course, but aren't we put here on this earth to bear each other's burdens? Does that mean Maggie has to learn how to bear *his* before he begins to bear hers? When he first met her, on almost the first night they spent together, she said to him in her theatrical way, "I'm a bitch, Ernest. I'm supposed to be one of the ten worst bitches in New York. I'll hurt you." But she has never hurt him, not deliberately. At least, he doesn't think so. She doesn't *mean* to torment him, if torment is the right word when he suffers no pain in the flesh. And he knows that none of his suffering is quite serious or real. Maggie will turn up sooner or later, and they may quarrel, but everything will turn out all right and she will fall asleep in his arms.

Ernest makes himself another Scotch and walks to the window to look down at the street, half thinking he may see Maggie getting out of a cab. At times, acting on premonition, he has walked to the window and seen just that. It is ten by now. There are few cars in sight. He goes into the kitchen, puts the dirty breakfast dishes in the sink, squirts Joy on them, and fills the sink with hot water.

The curious part of it all, he thinks as he does the dishes, is that he and Maggie, close as they are, have never been *really* involved. Not, at any rate, as he thinks true lovers must be. It isn't involvement with Maggie, but simply that they know each other through and through. Each knows what the other is going to do next, and accepts it, and comes back for more. God. If they were really involved, if what they did to each other had serious consequences, wouldn't this life have broken their hearts? There is something thin about both their pains and their pleasures— some pretense. His pain, waiting for Maggie, is mock pain, the kind you can half enjoy because you know it will not last. Ernest remembers playing a game they called "Tarzan" in the woods behind his house, when he was younger and weaker than the rest. He would be tied by his wrists to the branch of a tree that, when it sprang up, lifted him nearly off the ground. It hurt, and he was frightened each time, but his older brother, Charles, would be in the game, too, and Ernest knew that all he had to do was be patient until he was set free. He would wait quietly, his shoulders almost out of their sockets, for Charles to untie him. Once, before Charles came back for him, he fainted from the pain. It isn't the pain he remembers now or the fear; it is the excitement of waiting for Charles, of anticipating his release, of seeing Charles, his savior, slinking toward him through the trees. How much more real that game was than this! There is no real pain now. Maggie cannot really harm him, or really save him. Nor can he save her.

The dishes washed, Ernest lies down on the living-room sofa. He may be a fool, he thinks, but he is not the kind of fool people say he is. He isn't being victimized. His feelings aren't his to control, that's the trouble. Even at thirty-six, he can't handle them. But then how little experience he has had! He felt nothing at all—except in movies, sometimes—for years. With Maggie, he has been reborn.

Though it is no more than infatuation. He knows that. Aren't they both acting as if they were bewitched? This playing the same melodrama of betrayal and forgiveness over again and again! Isn't it like being under a spell? He once believed in magic, in spells. So did Maggie. He once believed in the divine wrath, when it comes to that. What if all this is a punishment visited upon him for not loving Paula, his wife, and upon Maggie for not loving Nat and her children? What if he and Maggie are *condemned* to go through this bitter, unreal suffering, over and over again? It is easier for him to see Maggie than to see himself, and it seems to him that she is compelled to defy him and hurt him in little ways, to taunt him to the point of leaving her, even though she is terrified of his leaving and of being left alone. Sometimes he thinks she wants him to be cruel to her, to give her pain.

Though he rarely strikes her, they have fights sometimes— passionate, violent ones—in which the voices that issue from their throats seem not their own but those of strangers. Maggie's becomes harsh and arrogant, his a whining child's. And through all the screaming and the imprecations they both keep calm and dry-eyed, as if they were no more than observers of the battle. And then they will listen to Puccini or Ravel or Rachmaninoff and, overcome by feeling for each other and for themselves, they will cry. Or something in them will cry. Through it all they remain detached in some way, he thinks. It frightens him, for it is as if they were possessed by devils. Maggie was born a Catholic, Ernest a Lutheran; there is a picture of hell-fire planted deep in their heads, along with the notion that marriage is a sacrament performed once and for all. In this day and age? He to Paula, God help him? Maggie, God help her, to Nat?

But what if it is true, Ernest thinks, that he and Maggie can only play at being lovers? What if one gets only a single chance? "How can you tell me you *love* me?" Maggie has cried more than once in that harsh voice that is not her own. "What's left to love? I'm a basket case. I'm damaged goods. What do you want to do? *Save* me? Do you think you're GOD?" And then she will throw him out of the house. She often throws him out of the house, and he will go, holding in his anger, careful not to leave cruel words hanging behind him in the air of the room. "I love you," he will call, and quickly close the door. Sometimes he will go back to the studio, but usually he will walk around the block and return. The chain will be on the door, and he will call through the crack until Maggie lets him in. She will be sitting in the kitchen wearing Nat's old maroon bathrobe and drinking straight Scotch. They will embrace after a time. If they are not too drunk by then, they will make love, and it will seem to Ernest that they are really touching, flesh to flesh.

At times, he is certain that Maggie is possessed—when she hears voices, or sees figures looming above their bed, or when she talks to the cat and the cat seems to talk back. And there was once when, naked and screaming, she pursued him down the hall to the door of the apartment and frightened him into turning on her, crossing himself, and raising one arm pointed straight at her with two fingers of his hand spread out, extended in the sign to ward off the evil eye. She cursed at him and spat and cowered back, hands crossed over her groin, trying to cover her nakedness. "You know the sign, do you?" she said in a flat voice. "Get out. Get out. Get out." He went back to the studio shivering—it was winter, and he left his coat behind—and reciting Hail Marys, words he did not know he knew. The next morning he called—"I think I forgot my coat," he said—and went over for breakfast. The storm had passed. Maggie remembered nothing, and it was as if nothing had happened at all.

Oh, we love each other, all right, Ernest thinks. Why try to analyze it away? How rare the bad scenes have been, after all. The worst is this anxious waiting, and even that is not so bad. Sometimes he thinks that if he had nothing, nothing at all, to be anxious about he would explode. Perhaps he stays with Maggie because of that, because she gives him something to be anxious over and releases him at the end. It's on the days after nights like this that he feels best and does his best work. It excites him to wait for her. Why would he do it if he didn't like it? She fills his mind. He is more aware of her now than he can be when she is there beside him—more excited by her. It *is* exciting, waiting for her and imagining where she may be.

He has tried not to—but what if, right now, he lets his imagination go? She is probably drinking with Fred what's-his-name, he knows that. They have been working off and on for the past two months on a pilot for one of Fred's clients. Maggie has talked about him. They have had drinks before. "He's no threat, Ernest," she has said. "He's gay." But how can he be sure Fred is entirely gay? Ernest has met him, at a party full of men who *were*—they were dancing, doing those campy tangos, all of that—but Fred was with a girl. Though she was the cold sort you'd expect him to be with if he was gay. Fred and the girl didn't stay long. Fred looked attractive but ruined. What if he were trying to go straight? Ernest knew a woman who told him the most proficient lover she'd ever had was gay. What if Maggie decided after three drinks she could help straighten Fred out? He lives in the Forties; it would be easy to go to his place. Why not? And then . . . But this is all so unlikely, Ernest thinks. Maggie never lets herself go that far, or if she does and sleeps with anyone else it's a mistake. Literally a mistake. She has to be drunk enough to think it's him. He remembers coming up to the apartment one Saturday afternoon after she had been shopping with a visiting client from Chicago, buying presents for his wife and children. She answered the door weeping, her hair in her eyes, her dress torn. "He raped me," she sobbed. "The bastard *raped* me. I thought it was you."

Ah, it is true. The waiting makes her more real. He wants her now. Where is she? In Fred's arms? *Under* him? Too drunk to know what she is doing? Thinking that faggot is *me*? How strange she is, Ernest thinks. Terrified of rape, she says, and yet she wears no more than those little dresses and in the summer hardly anything else at all. "I remember when I was young," she will say. "Can you believe it? Without a girdle, I used to feel *naked*." And when passion does strike her it is sudden, like a windstorm off the prairie. It happens so fast and is over so fast—

hardly enough to call it fucking, hardly enough to call it an act. A quick sigh, and that's all. Thinking of it, Ernest remembers driving up a hill with Maggie in winter, in a rented car. The road was covered with thin ice and the tires slipped back so that they could only inch up slowly, slowly, waiting, hoping they would get to the top. Maggie could not bear it, the tension of waiting was too great, and got out of the car. He had to come back down for her once he'd reached the top, sliding on foot down the hill. Pines on either side, light snow on the road, the sky clear and blue, an inn at the top of the hill where, finally, they sat and drank. Maggie could never bear waiting, or slow love.

Ernest makes himself a cup of coffee. Now it is half past ten. Maggie will be back before long, and he wants his mind to be clear. Another drink could put him in a jealous rage. God knows, he thinks, we both take *some* strange pleasure in this. He hopes the pleasure does not spoil; it did with his wife. When she called the other day about the alimony check he'd forgotten to send, he told her more about his life with Maggie than he meant to. He usually does. "Does it ever occur to you that you and Maggie have interlocking neuroses?" Paula said. *Occur* to him? How else—why else—do people get together in this vale of tears! What else binds people together at all? That and blood, and loyalty sometimes. Isn't it worth it? I *need* someone to wait for, Ernest thinks, and I need to know she will return. With Paula, he was never sure she would return. And Paula is hard. Maggie has never come to terms with the world; she is innocent and vulnerable. Maggie's vulnerability is what makes it so difficult, for Ernest knows that some day he will have to leave her for good—go beyond her, beyond these games and this waiting. He will have to begin to change. "You think life is a Broadway play," he has said to Maggie. "For you, the characters never change; they go through their paces, that's all. But life is a novel. It has to be. People have to change."

"People don't change," Maggie has said to him. "Only characters in novels."

But there is change, Ernest thinks, if there is life.

Sitting in the kitchen now, Ernest makes himself another cup of coffee. Waiting! he thinks. Lord, *how* they were made to wait, he and his brother, by the women in the family, their grandmother and their aunts. Charles, less patient than he, had a sharper tongue, but he was intimidated by those women, too. "Wait here, children," Grandmother would say. "Wait right here. I'll only be a minute." And Charles, smirking and raising his eyebrows, would whisper, "That means at least an *hour*."

"Wait in the car. I'll be right back," she would say.

"Oh, mercy, I forgot my purse," she would say. "Run in, Charles, and get it like a good boy. No. No. I'd better get it myself. You children wait."

"Wait till your grandmother starts eating, Ernest. Put that fork down."

"No, you may *not* be excused. You sit right there until everybody else has finished his dessert."

What tyrants they were! And if you made *them* wait! If you were five minutes late for dinner or dawdled in the bath on Sunday before church! Ah, those Sundays of waiting! Sitting in Sunday school. Sitting in church. Waiting for Sunday dinner until all the folks had arrived. Sitting in the car during Grandma's Sunday drive. Waiting through the long afternoon, when all he and Charles were permitted was quiet play. Waiting for supper. Waiting for the popcorn after supper. Going to bed not tired enough for sleep and waiting for sleep. No wonder he and Charles had Sunday headaches to this day.

Shopping with their grandmother was the worst. "Just a few more minutes, children. Grandma has to buy a few more things." *Has* to buy! As if duty and nothing else impelled her to try on those frocks! He and Charles would sit in the mahogany-panelled ladies' waiting room on a bench without cushions that stood against the wall next to the bathroom and not far from the store's cashier. Money and sales slips came to her cage from every floor through tubes that ran in a cluster near the ceiling. Blackstone's was the largest department store in southern Indiana, seven stories high. Cartridges dropped into a basket inside the cage. *Whoosh*, then *thup*. *Whoosh-whoosh*. *Thup*. *Thup*. Call bells rang. *Ping*. Pause. *Ping*. Pause. *Ping ping*. Smell of furniture oil and lilac disinfectant. The faint rush of water in the toilets. And the women. Out they stepped, out of the elevators, out the ladies-room door. Swish of skirts. Swish of stockings on heavy thighs. Plump Indiana farm women. He and Charles would discuss, giggling, what they must look like when they took off their clothes. Like the ladies on the girdle pages in the Sears catalog? Like Grandma? But she was all skin and bones. Ernest remembers seeing her in her corset one day, seeing her brown leathery flesh. Why was she so brown? Was that why she ordered those creams all the way from Marshall Field's in Chicago—to make her skin light? He and Charles discussed these things without passion—unless their dry, insistent curiosity had passion—and never talked about them much except when they were waiting on that hard bench, waiting, waiting, having to keep still and with nothing, really nothing at all, to do. Then a louder bell than the call bells would ring, and it would mean there was only half an hour until closing, and then the fifteen-minute bell rang, and finally their grandmother would come and they would leave the store on the last elevator, going out to the parking lot past men waiting to lock the doors behind them. And then their grandmother would drive the fifty miles home while they sat in the back of the car, waiting to be out of there and free.

Then Charles was in long trousers and allowed to stay behind while Ernest went with his grandmother to Blackstone's alone, and then Ernest was in long trousers, too. "My baby's growing up," his grandmother had said when she saw him. She had pretended to cry, and then she had really cried. She had taken the boys from their father after their mother died. Wasn't she better qualified to bring up children after raising five of her own? But she hadn't wanted *them,* she wanted her daughter back, and what she saw in her grandsons were remembrances of their mother—fragments and vestiges she did her best to preserve. "That's just what Mary would do," she would say as she watched Charles open a Christmas present, unloosening the knot instead of breaking the cord, folding the paper neatly. Or she would say to Ernest, "You were sleeping the way your mother did when I tucked you in last night." Sometimes, when they sat in the living room in the evening after dinner, Ernest would look up and see his grandmother staring at him or at Charles, staring through them at something in the past before they were born. It was an eerie feeling. As if they were expected to *become* their mother, as if they were only real when they were like her. No wonder Charles had turned queer. The wonder was that he, Ernest, hadn't joined him. And their father— when they saw him, which wasn't often—was no help. He expected the same. Half their blood was their mother's and that was the half he wanted to see. He liked them studious and gentle and they had complied.

Ernest turned out to be the image of his mother, and how they had spoiled him! Dolling him up, slicking down his hair! Charles, feeling ignored, began to grow bitter and mean, while Ernest became everyone's darling. And he was to be *preserved.* He was to take no risks. He could not ride bicycles or swim or skate on the river ice or have a dog. Dogs got rabies. He was to stay alive.

They brought him up, Ernest can see now, as if he were a girl. Those fantasies he had of being transformed into a beautiful princess! Never into a prince. He knew he was a boy and that he would have to grow up to be a man, and he half resented it. His soul was female, trapped in a boy's body. Even now, when Ernest remembers his fantasies, his body warms and an easy lassitude begins to overcome him, like that he occasionally feels after making love. Perhaps that is why he sometimes has the notion after making love with Maggie that they have each taken on the sex of the other for a moment and have become whole and at peace. And his later fantasies were never of seducing women and conquering them, but of rescuing them, of being near them, hearing their talk, seeing them dress and make up, touching them, touching their clothes, smelling their perfumes. He remembers his aunts' closets, remembers sitting in them, remembers trying on their clothes. . . . He has still, he thinks, a feminine soul. Of course he doesn't mind waiting. He waits as a woman waits, to be filled.

But now there comes to him the memory of waiting for his father, whom he does not love, on those weekends not long after his mother's death when his father drove down from Chicago to visit his sons. It was Ernest who waited and not Charles. Charles was nine and had a life of his own. Ernest was five. He would wait quietly through the long Saturday afternoons, sitting on the concrete steps outside his grandmother's house, waiting for his father's green Chevrolet. On the porch was a creaking swing, painted dark gray, that hung from hooks in the light-gray ceiling. Its motion made Ernest's head ache and he never sat in it long. He preferred the steps and sat there, shaded by the trees on each side of the walk, looking for his father's car, trying to discover it coming far down the road, knowing that it would not appear before dinnertime but waiting there from three o'clock on, unable to do anything but wait.

And then his father would arrive and there would be presents and a quick hug, and that night he and his father would sleep in the same bed. His father would snore and Ernest would lie awake listening to the snoring. His father wore brown pajamas with yellow frogs and a Chinese character on the pocket that stood, his father said, for either "Long Life" or "Happiness." His father smelled of cigarettes and Listerine and Lifebuoy soap, and in the morning he would shave with his electric razor. His silver pen and pencil and his leather wallet and his notebook would be on Ernest's dresser. The electric alarm clock his father brought would wake them early, so that his father could play golf before church on the nine-hole course south of town. Charles would go with him around the course and Ernest would wait for them at home, wait for the moment when his father returned, smelling a little of whiskey and sweat, and lifted him up in his arms and rubbed his cheek, scratchy in spite of his shaving, against Ernest's own.

And how much waiting there has been after that! Waiting to grow up, waiting to go to college, waiting to leave Indiana for good, waiting to get out of the Army, waiting to live in New York City, waiting to feel love, waiting . . .

How weak it makes him sound. Ernest knows it. Only the weak have to wait. Waiting is the penalty inflicted upon the weak by the strong. But it is hardly a harsh penalty, Ernest thinks. He, waiting, is happier than Maggie, who has made him wait. Wherever she is, he knows that by this hour—it is going on twelve—she would rather be at home with him. Waiting, he escapes from time in a way. It no longer passes so quickly but hangs heavy, making him a present of itself. One hour becomes three, and his life, spent largely in waiting, seems endlessly long.

What are the times of waiting? Why, adolescence, when one waits for freedom and for love, and old age, when one waits for death. The experts in waiting, Ernest thinks, are the old and those who, like himself, have never left adolescence behind, who were never led out of it and into the world. They can wait with something like patience, openly and without shame, because they have nothing in particular to do. There was no one to take him out of his adolescence in that house full of women—his father, by the time Ernest was ready, had given up trying—and no one to introduce him to the world. He has had to become his own guide. He is awkward and lazy at it still, and he knows it, but he will find his way out of this prison in time. He believes that, and knows he is in a prison. He does not intend to spend all his life waiting. Though he may love her—if it is love—he knows he will leave Maggie behind. But not yet.

The doorbell rings, and Ernest goes to the refrigerator for the daisies. When he comes out of the kitchen, he sees that Maggie has already let herself in and is standing stock-still in the hallway, feet apart, her shoes and bag in her hands, her coat on the floor at her feet.

"That bastard," she says. "That bastard."

"Hey, Maggie," Ernest says, holding up the daisies before her. "Hey. Look. I got you some flowers!"

"Oh, Ernest, aren't they *lovely!*" Maggie says. She has been beaten. On the left side of her face is a great bruise. Blood stains the collar of her dress. To Ernest, she is terrifying and beautiful. Her eyes are bright.

The Old Glory

They came down the winding sand-worn stairs from South Shore Drive to the powerhouse road, the whole lot of them, all the Peckhams from miles around strung out behind Gran Peckham, who puffed and snorted, a dingy woodburning loco-motive, as she led them down the ninety-seven white steps. James Peckham, who had found his own way down along a path half grown over with brier bushes, crouched behind scrub maple at the road's edge watching his clan descend through the smoke-blue air, each of them looming out of the dusk just above him, one after another, Peckham after Peckham, with a sprink-ling of in-laws and cousins, some with kinder faces and softer names, Miller or Symonds or Read.

James was nine and the youngest of Gran Peckham's grand-children. There were great-grandchildren older than he, and he had first cousins more than twice his age. His father had been born a good ten years after Gran had given up thought of having another child, and turned out thin-blooded and thin-skinned; some of this had come down to his son. James was spindly and precocious, and already had the stooped, worn look of his father, with a nose too big for his face, close-set squinting eyes, and thin black hair he kept slicked down with Vaseline. He had been living in the town with his grandparents for only a few months, and this, the Independence Day holiday, was the first time since he had come that he had seen all the family together. So much had gone on during the day that he had run off finally, after the picnic and the oratory and the ball games, to walk the beach and the bluffs alone, happy to be by himself and quiet for a while before the fireworks began. He feared the fireworks, feared their glare and noise.

It was hardly the town or the family or the occasion the boy would have chosen, but the choice was not his. Just the previous winter, on a cold, starry February night, he had seen from the observation gallery at the Newark airport the plane on which his mother and father were returning from Miami touch ground, veer, nose over, and unaccountably burst into flames. It was an hour before the fire was put out. Neither of his parents survived.

What was to become of the orphan was perhaps too quickly settled. Gran Peckham, who at seventy-eight ruled her family as sternly as she had a generation before, came from Michigan to New York for the funeral, the only Peckham there. After the funeral, when the relatives gathered for supper in the apartment on East Eighty-third Street that had been the boy's home since he was born, the old woman asserted her claim upon her grandson. No other claim, as it turned out, was made, and although the aunts and uncles on his mother's side had little use for the Peckhams, putting the boy in his grandmother's hands seemed the only sensible thing to do. So James went back with her to live in Fair Harbor, on Lake Michigan, in the yellow stucco house on the edge of town that his grandparents had built not long after they were married, years before the First World War, the drafty old house where his father and his father's brothers and sisters had been born and brought up, and where his grandmother, since her husband's death nearly fifteen years before, had been living alone.

The boy didn't have much of a life there. He missed his parents terribly. Since their death he had grown timid, shrinking from whatever was too loud or too bright, taking no chances, avoiding any contest, any show of force. Clear night skies, even, set him to worrying, for these were the times when unforeseen disasters might happen. When the skies were clear, he wished with all his heart for rain. When he was awake the question for which he could find no answer— Why did it happen to me?— circled around and around in his brain. On the edge of sleep he would see and hear again the crash and the blazing wreck in which his mother and father had died. Asleep, he would be wakened by dreams he could not remember. He was called lazy, but he was busy enough.

The old woman, in her brusque way, tried to bring James out of his shell, though nothing seemed to help much. He was tractable and did as he was told, but he never kept to one thing for long. Nor did he care much for those his own age—perhaps because he couldn't yet spare the time from his brooding, perhaps because he felt he now had little in common with the young. "You'll be an old man before you're a little boy," his grandmother would say to him in exasperation. She was probably right. Only one person, Gran's last surviving brother, James's great-uncle Ned, had been able to draw close to him, though there was not much they could share. The boy spoke seldom, the old man only to say what he had already said many times. But they had become friends.

James liked to wander about the town on his own, and by now nearly everyone, Peekham or no, knew him and saw to it that he didn't get into trouble, giving him lunch if he turned up at midday or a ride home if it was getting late. They called him Old James—ironically, perhaps, because of the difference between his age and that of the other Peckhams, or because the older people in town saw the strong resemblance between the boy and his father, who had had the same name.

In June, James had even wandered off from his own birthday party, which, as the town wag said, really took the cake, candles and all. It had been a surprise party, a last effort by the Peckham family to make him feel at home, an all-day outing on a farm belonging to Albert Peckham, Gran's eldest son, to which the boys in James's class were invited. They had been given the run of the place—scrambling around in the hayloft, paddling in the brackish pond, hallooing through the back woods along a treasure trail laid by one of the Peckham men the day before. In all of this James took his noisy part for most of the day, while his grandmother and the women clucked their approval. But in the middle of the afternoon he disappeared, which was bad enough, and left the pasture gate open behind him, which was worse, for it freed the lone Peckham cow. It was the middle of June, just after the close of school; the apple trees were in full blossom, and picnic tables had been spread in the grove just back of the house. The boys, still frenzied from their chase through the woods, set up a caterwauling *corrida* and so harried the poor cow that she plunged finally into the apple grove, bellowing, shaking the white petals down upon her, and butting over one of the tables before Albert Peckham could get to her and calm her down.

James missed it all. An hour or so later he reappeared, his shoes muddy from walking along the creek that cut through the lower pasture, his trousers torn in going over the barbed-wire fence. The women had reset the table, the cow was at her ease again in a far corner of the pasture, and the boys, sick from too much laughter, were sprawled like exhausted infantrymen under the trees. No one made a sound. James walked up and sat next to his great-uncle Ned, who was red-faced from the laughing and the strain.

"Well," the boy said cheerily, with a try at playing the good fellow, "what have you all been up to now?"

That was enough to set them off, hooting and screaming, holding their bellies, doubling up with laughter. Bewildered, James first tried to join in. Then he understood that they were laughing at him, and for no reason that he knew he began to cry. He did his best to make them think the sobs that shook him were the throes of laughter, but Uncle Ned must have known, for he took James inside and saw to it that he washed his hands and face. They were all quite kind, really; after all, it was his birthday. The incident did nothing to change the boy's ways, and he continued to keep to himself as he had before. The Peckhams gave up trying to make anything of him but what he was, and left him pretty much to his own devices. Except on the Fourth of July. There, on that family occasion, as the youngest grandchild and as substitute for his father—Gran Peckham, indeed, sometimes seemed to confuse the boy with her dead son—James was expected to play his part.

There had been a fireworks display on the south beach every Fourth of July night since the turn of the century, when Fair Harbor, now a shabby, half-forgotten resort on the eastern shore of Lake Michigan, had been a summer home for well-to-do families from St. Louis and Chicago. Like the town, the display seemed less elegant than it had been, but few thought of missing it, even so. Aside from the Memorial Day observances at the cemetery and the Cherry Festival this was the only grand community occasion left.

The Peckham family had watched the fireworks from the roof of the town filtration plant, a windowless concrete structure about twenty feet high, ever since the plant was built, right next to the powerhouse, in the early thirties. Bud Peckham, Gran's second son, had been night engineer at the powerhouse for all that time, so it was easy for the family to go through the powerhouse and up to the adjoining roof, and soon their exclusive right to the roof was an accepted thing. At first only a few Peckhams came, just those living in the town and nearby, but after most of Gran's children had married and moved away, the

Fourth replaced Christmas as the time for the family to come together. Bringing the children was easier in the summer, and besides nearly everyone wanted to spend the Christmas holidays at home, with their own tree. By now the small children were of the third generation and the young parents were ready to spend the Fourth, too, in some other way, but they deferred to the old woman's implacable sense of family ceremony, and came —so many of them that the Peckhams in the town had trouble finding enough room to put everyone up. The ritual, overladen by now, was about ready to fall of its own weight, and only Gran Peckham kept it alive, as it may have kept her alive, year after year—bound and determined to see one more family Fourth. Until she was dead most of the family would continue to come.

This year the day had been pretty much like last year and the years before. Early that morning an advance guard had appeared at Beechwood Park on the bluffs south of town carrying most of the provisions and all the softball gear, in plenty of time to commandeer the best diamond and enough picnic tables to go around. The diamond was busy from then until the last of the Peckhams left in the early evening, first with shagging flies, then with workup as more players came along, and then with the team games—fathers vs. sons, girls vs. boys, oldsters vs. youngsters, husbands vs. wives.

By noon, nearly everyone was there and people began to eat. The picnic went on for some time; in fact, it never really stopped. The old ones sat around the tables long after everyone else had left, piecing at the chicken carcasses and what was left of the baked hams, drinking lemonade or beer or ice tea, and talking over the year. Except for the diehard ball players, the others wandered off, not too far, into the pine woods or down to the beach below, some for a cap-gun battle, some for tree tag or red light, some for gossip, some for kissing, some merely to get away. A few went in the water, though it was still cold. James, who had hung about with Uncle Ned at home most of the morning and come out with him in the last car, was ready to stay at the table with the old men and listen to their talk, but they teased him and shooed him away, calling him Old James. He went off then to the woods, angry at being teased, and joined his Chicago cousins, the most rambunctious of them all, who had smuggled a hoard of firecrackers into town. They ran down the beach and fired them off. Just then, James liked the noise.

At half past three, nearly everyone was back again for the band concert in the weathered green pavilion that stood in the center of the park. Before the concert began, Gran Peckham, with James standing beside her to help, handed each of the children as they filed past her a small American flag. Then the Peckham children all marched over together, a ragged column, to occupy the front rows of the benches ranged on three sides of the pavilion. James found a seat among them, squeezed between cousins, his flag clutched in his fist, cricking his neck to see what he could of the players in the band.

The program had been the same for years. First "The Star-Spangled Banner," while everyone stood at attention singing. Then the "Washington Post" and "El Capitan" marches, and "In a Persian Garden," and a medley of patriotic airs. And then "God Bless America" while they all stood and sang again. The mayor spoke and someone read a telegram from the governor, who had not been able to come, and then the Declaration of Independence was read by the girl who had been high school valedictorian in the spring, and the boy who had won the junior-high declamation contest recited, in singsong measured phrases, the Gettysburg Address: ". . . We are met on a great battle-field of that war. We have come to dedicate a portion of that field, as a final resting place for those who here gave their lives that that nation might live. It is altogether fitting and proper that we should do this. . . ." James listened, seeing a bent, bearded Lincoln before a hushed crowd and imagining scenes of carnage, of soldiers' bloody deaths. Afterward, while the band played "The Stars and Stripes Forever" and then played it again, the children stood waving their flags in time with the conductor's baton until, as was bound to happen, someone started an impromptu strutting, tootling parade that wound through the park for a while until it turned into a game of follow-the-leader and was lost in the woods.

The day grew hotter. While the smallest children napped or suckled in the shade, the softball began in earnest and went on through the long afternoon, game after game. The air was muggy, with not a breath of wind, and by late afternoon everyone was tired and dusty and ready to drop. People began to break away, off to one house or another for a little supper and the chance to stretch out for forty winks before the time came to assemble again for the fireworks. It had been just too much of a day.

James felt as tired as the rest. He had been caught up in the day's flurry, drawn willy-nilly into more of the games and chatter than at first he had had a mind for. And he had had a better time than he expected, though it was still work for him to play. But he went off finally after a bad showing as shortstop in the third inning of the oldster-youngster game, to walk back alone toward town along the beach, where he could keep clear of the rest of the family until the fireworks began. Not far from the powerhouse he stretched out on the sand in the shade cast now by the low dunes and fell asleep. When he woke up hungry an hour or so later he went over to the refreshment stand near the pier and successfully begged for a hot dog and a candy apple, for he had no money. Then he climbed up to explore the bluffs above until it began to grow dark.

Now at dusk he watched the Peckham clan descend the stairs one by one, men and women and children and babies in arms, and counted them as they came like freight cars at a crossing. Fifty-one. Fifty-two. Fifty-three. No, fifty-four. His Uncle Ned appeared out of the gloom, with his beard, his belly, his cane, and his checkerboard cap, trailing behind like an unhitched caboose. James broke from cover and ran up to walk beside him. It was a moment before the old man, startled, knew who it was. "I thought you'd turn up," he said. "That's what I told Gran."

The two of them fell in at the end of the procession, moving slowly behind the others down the cindertop road toward the powerhouse and the filtration plant, above them to the right the sand bluff and the empty town, to their left the populous beach, glowing with sparklers and weenie-roast fires, then the lake, the two piers with their slowly turning lights, and, far out, the clouded horizon. Gran Peckham, with one of the men at her elbow, went on ahead to see that everything was all right. The other grownups clustered to talk or share a nip while outriding children galloped up and down the line or flung themselves, giggling with a last frenzied burst of high spirits, to scuffle in the still-warm sand. James stayed behind with the old man, ready to make a getaway with him into the dunes, some place where they could sit together for a few minutes in the violet air. They were to be at Gran Peckham's right and left hand throughout the fireworks, and neither of them liked the prospect much.

The Coast Guard bell on one of the piers sounded four times. "In here," James said, tugging his great-uncle by the hand toward a little valley between two low dunes. He made a path for the old man, holding back the beach grass that grew waist-high before them. After a few yards they came to a clearing that opened southwestward toward a part of the beach they could not see from the road. The stretch of beach before them was empty. They sat down, hidden from the road by the high grass, and looked out together at the lake. It was cloudier down that way. There were only a few small lights, red and yellow, and now and then a flare of heat lightning far off to the south. The air was still.

"Rain's coming," the old man said, easing himself a seat in the sand.

"Tonight?" James asked. If only it could rain right now, he thought, there would be no fireworks and he would be free to go his own way, untroubled by the family or the glare of the rockets and their noise.

"By midnight most likely. Maybe before."

The old man pulled out a pack of cigarettes from the breast pocket of his blue jacket, extricated one, and lit it carefully, his hands trembling. The boy leaned over and blew out the match. "I always rolled my own," the old man said, "until the stroke. Then I lost so much damn tobacco there was nothing to do. I used to sit there in bed working at it with the tobacco piling up in front of me like lathe shavings. Then Doc told me to quit acting like a fool."

The mosquitoes were getting worse. The old man lit two sticks of punk and stuck them upright in the sand. James had saved some of the supply of firecrackers his Chicago cousins had given him in the afternoon. Now he lit a sparkler from one of the sticks of punk and whirled it slowly, liking the metallic smell, wishing for rain.

"It was a funny thing," the old man said. "I was getting the stepladder out from the garage, there at Gran's place. Gran had said the eaves-trough on the back porch wasn't draining properly and the drip was spoiling the pansy border. I told her I'd take a look the next time I was over; it wasn't so high. Most likely leaves in the drainpipe or a ball from one of the kids playing anty-i-over, but I didn't even get the ladder off the garage wall. I don't know how it happened. It felt like a light bulb burst inside my head."

It had happened many years ago and James had heard the story many times. He said nothing, but whirled his sparkler, chanting to himself, bringing on the rain.

"I used to play a lot of chess then. There was nobody in town that played a good game, though old Mr. Jenner wasn't too bad when he set his mind to it, so I used to play with people all over the world, by mail. Some games took years. I tried to keep it up for a while afterward, but I couldn't remember. I got the games all mixed up. I used to have all the games in my head, and I'd play them out in the evenings when there wasn't much to do. I wrote everybody finally and told them it was no use, I couldn't remember any more."

The boy had nothing to say, and the old man fell silent too. They sat there together looking out at the rain clouds that were now moving slowly toward them, riding on the soft wind from the prairies.

"I've got a two-incher here," said James. "Let's shoot it off."

"Best not," Uncle Ned said, but the boy had touched the cracker to the punk and cast it down the sand dune below them. Short-fused, it burst brightly in the air, slapping their eardrums sharply, holding them for half a second in a cold blaze of white. The old man winced, his bent legs contracting like a frog's in the pan. "Damn," he said. "Better come along." Blind for a moment, he felt in the sand for his stick, then pushed himself to his feet. The boy's eyes, until the flash, had been clinging to the afterglow in the western sky. But now when his sight returned the sky seemed pitch black. The voices from the big beach were nearly still. He stumbled back with the old man through the tall grass, for the way they had come in by was lost.

They stood at the road's edge getting used to the dark. Filaments of spiderweb clung to the boy's face and tickled his nostrils. Through the murmuring of the crowd on the beach he could hear the clang of the bell-buoy and the wash of waves against the south pier. The rain now seemed far away. Everything around him seemed far away.

Now they crunched along the cindertop road, two-legs and three-legs, toward the great open door of the powerhouse that slashed a yellow parallelogram out of the night. The others had all gone ahead and they had the road to themselves. From somewhere before them the Coast Guard bell rang again, five times, and over the last clang the boy heard a choked thud out on the lake that must mark the beginning. "One. Two. Three." Uncle Ned counted the seconds aloud. Then a quick ball of white light, high above the piers, and a breath later the concussion, echoing tinnily from the lake, the clouds, the brick and concrete, striking James in the chest lightly with an invisible fist. From the crowd came a sigh in which the two on the road involuntarily joined. It was what they had been waiting for. "They're about to start," the old man said. "Best move right along."

The beach came alive with voices. Above them all the boy heard, some distance away, a yipping dog. The Coast Guard klaxon sounded, then the firehouse siren from the town and a concert of whistles from the factories to the south. A motorboat roared blindly down the river between the piers and out into the lake. "Crazy fools," the old man said.

The boy found it was the waiting that troubled him more than the noise. He would have run the rest of the way now, but held back, walking slowly beside the old man toward the power-house door.

Bud Peckham sat inside, cocked back in a mahogany captain's chair under the bare work lights, some magazine or other splayed upon his belly, his feet in black ankle-high shoes not quite touching the cement floor. "Pretty late," was all he said.

They climbed the grilled iron stairs slowly, with the high hum of the dynamos in their ears. The boy peered down beneath his feet at the machinery, dull red and shining brass, in the dim pit below. It was hot and close at the top. Looking down at the dynamos, the range of dials, the boilers, and the piping, the boy felt a cloud pass over his eyes and his brain. For a moment he thought he must throw himself down into the inexplicable source of energy that lay below. The moment passed.

Reluctant to join the others, they waited at the top of the stairs to hear the signal of the next skyburst. "No hurry," the old man said. "As lief be hung for a sheep as a lamb." Then the sound came to them, more a vibration of the metal platform on which they stood than any movement of the air. James pushed open the heavy door and they crossed over the footbridge to the filtration-plant roof.

And now all the Peckhams were gathered again, for the last time that year, the older ones ranged on slatted funeral-parlor chairs, the younger ones leaning against the low parapet that encircled the roof or sprawled out on army blankets thrown on the concrete. "Jimmy, come on over here! There's room," one of his cousins called from the darkness. "Can't," the boy said. He wished he could.

They were a good two stories above the rest of the crowd on top of the structure into which the town's water was pumped from the lake to find its way through layers of gravel and sand before being pumped again up to a standpipe on the hills to the east. The throb of the pumps made the roof vibrate, not un-pleasantly, nothing like the nervous whirr in the powerhouse. Those massed on the beach below, couple by couple, family by family, seemed remote and unfortunate. From the roof, from the seats of honor, the view was superb.

Gran Peckham was sitting alone in front of the company, a dark shadow of uncompromising flesh. There was an empty chair on each side of her. The old man and the boy, trying to slip in quietly beside her, were transfixed by the light of the first slowly parachuting magnesium flare. Gran gave little sign of recognition, except to settle more firmly in her seat with a fem-inine rustling that seemed out of keeping with her size and her age. In the glare James could see that her cheeks were rouged high on the bone, and her lips were a taut magenta bow. She held her twisted hands knotted together upon her lap, loose envelopes of flesh drooped from her chin, her eyes were pock-eted deep in tawny hummocks. She sat erect, squat, unmoved, looking as if she cared for nothing except that she was there still, for one more year, with the others behind her and the old man and the boy at her side. She was part Potawatomi, people said, from the north, from around Manistee. James wondered for a moment what she must have seen and what she saw now through those buried eyes.

There the two ancients and the boy sat, each trying to make sure that the ceremony, such as it was, went off well. Their chairs, set at an angle apart from the rest, faced toward a barge moored about two hundred yards off-shore from which the fireworks would be launched. To those seated behind them they appeared in half profile, lit erratically by the hovering fires above. James understood that he had, this once, to take on the dignity of his elders, to assert by his bearing, so far as he might, that the Peckham line maintained in him its dignity and its strength. It was not easy for him. In the hours since he had left the park and the games, his old anxieties had returned. He was afraid, knowing at the same time there could hardly be anything to fear. He wished there were, wished for some real catastrophe—war or tornado or earthquake—that might test his courage. What was so hard was just to sit as he knew he must, with that show of calm that seemed to come so easily to the two beside him. Accustomed to slouching in parlor chair or pew, easily set aflutter by spectacle and noise, James now braced himself, feet twisted about his chair's front legs, hands clasped tightly in his lap, a pale copy of the woman at his side. He envied the other children sitting back there out of sight chattering in the shadows, yet he felt a kind of pride at being where he was.

As the boy tried to conceal his youth and his fears, the old man tried to conceal his frailty. It was no easier. He suffered from palsy, as he had since his stroke, but by placing his stick across his knees and clutching it hard he could nearly control the trembling, although the pain it gave the muscles of his hands was enough to bring tears to his eyes. For the old woman, it was probably not so hard. The strength left in her came not from the momentary exercise of will but from habits long practiced, so long that it seemed to all of her family that she must have been, although she was not, to her stern manner born.

Five bright flares suddenly appeared above the crowd upon the beach and floated down, drifting, casting wild shadows. James looked at the old couple beside him. It was as if he could see through their flesh to the bones of their knuckles, their skulls, the sockets of their eyes. They are as tired as I am, he thought, and they must be very old.

Then it was dark, as dark as the far side of the moon, nearly as soundless. Out on the lake the boy saw a jagged orange path of light, a torch moving on the barge. There were several soft explosions, then several more. With everyone else, he looked up. The sky filled with jeweled flowers—ruby, emerald, sapphire, amethyst—and then a cascade of glittering diamonds that seemed flung down from somewhere deep in space. Then there was nothing, the night had swallowed it all.

After a long wait, so long the boy was certain something had gone wrong on the barge, a single rocket traced a dotted line up into the air, where it burst hollowly, much lower than the others had been, and threw out a handful of blue tendrils that fell slowly until they faded just above the crowd. Again there was a pause—heat lightning flashed along the southerly horizon— and again a rocket, not much better than the last. They must have used up all their good ones, the boy thought, in the first round.

The next piece rose hissing in a clean arc to a point nearly above his head and then scattered, in a series of muffled bursts, a bunch of chrysanthemums, yellow and red and blue, and, when he thought it was over, with a sharp crack, a flurry of green stars. Then another went up, to explode into purple. And then another, into red. And then a rocket whose first gold bloom, fading more quickly this time, exploded into one larger, and that into one still larger again.

By now, James had forgotten both himself and his fear. He

had forgotten to think of the coming rain. Whoever it was that controlled the display, working in darkness upon the barge, had come to command him wholly, at least for the time—both his passions and his brain. Upon the boy, as upon fire's explosive force, the unknown artist had imposed a kind of order, a kind of calm.

One by one, slowly, the rockets continued to ascend. The boy found it no longer enough just to admire them. Something in the rhythm of their sequence led him to discover what he thought was a design in their firing, and this led him toward more pleasure in what he saw. He began to judge and to compare, to applaud silently what he thought a master stroke, to say to himself now and then that it might have been better done.

Perhaps the display went on too long, for some in the crowd began an insistent clapping, then others took it up, urging on the finale. But the master of the fires, who was after all out of earshot, kept to his tempo and his plan. Once, twice, three times, rockets rose crazily in an eccentric path to fizzle and plunge, without bursting, into the water. There were catcalls from the crowd below. Then the next rocket, sent up with a charge louder than the rest, rose majestically and exploded with a grand crash, hurling out tourbillions of color that changed all at once into floating, dancing balls of fire. James, forgetting the solemn role he had set out to play, clapped his hands. And suddenly there was pandemonium, a drunken fury of explosions, and a sky filled with stars, jewels, blooms, fountains, comets, cascades, fingers of light—spendthrift fires that flourished and died and were succeeded, it seemed endlessly, by as many again. Then a salvo of sharp concussions, until the boy felt himself gasp for breath. Then there was nothing left in the sky but a lone red flare, and when he looked again that too was gone. It was over.

"Look!" the boy cried. "Look there!" He unkinked his legs from the chair and bent forward, hand on his grandmother's arm. The lake before them was turning into fire. A sheet of incandescent white flame that rustled like corn in the wind spread out southward from the pier, doubled by its reflection in the quiet inshore water. For a moment it was bright as day. Leaning over the parapet he could see people gathering up their things, moving away from the beach, going home. He could smell the rain.

Now upon the pier itself, traced sketchily in ribbons of red, and white, and blue fire, its upper left corner sparkling with artificial stars, there flickered the biggest American flag James had ever seen. Once more a bomb burst high above them.

"It's Old Glory, James," his grandmother said, leaning toward him. "Now it's all over." She got slowly to her feet.

The boy got up too. He felt unsteady. The old woman drew him to her for a moment; she smelled of lavender and dust. "Please take my arm, James," she said. "We must go down now and say our goodbyes."

"Starting to rain," Uncle Ned said. He began to rise from his chair.

The three of them made their way toward the powerhouse stairs as the others stood aside to let them pass. It was quiet now, except for a baby's whimper and the click and clatter as the men folded the chairs.

James, grasping the old woman's arm firmly as he had been taught to do, guided her across the footbridge and down the iron stairs, slowly, a step at a time, while she panted and wheezed, vexed a little, he supposed, because now she needed his help. The old man followed behind. At the bottom of the stairs they stopped just inside the open powerhouse door. Gran Peckham sat down, quite out of breath, in the mahogany captain's chair where Bud had sat. The old man and the boy stood beside her, one on each side. James looked down at his grandmother, appearing small and withered now in the big chair under the yellow lights.

The others began to come down the stairs, filing past, one by one, to say goodbye, raising their voices enough to be heard over the whirring dynamos. The sons and daughters, their wives and husbands, grandchildren and great-grandchildren, nephews and nieces. Some bent over Gran to kiss her cheek or stopped to joke with the old man. Goodbye. Goodbye now. Come see us if you can. Until next year, yes, next year. Goodbye.

No one stopped for long. The cement floor of the power-house sloped sharply there down to the door; that and the press from those still on the stairs made the line move a little faster than anyone intended. It was just as well. They were all in a hurry to get home now before the heavy rain.

James, along with Gran Peckham and Uncle Ned, said goodbye to them all. Perhaps because he had the advantage of the inclined floor, perhaps because he was holding himself more erect than he had, the boy felt tall, and less weary than he had expected. He shook the hand of each cousin, each uncle, each aunt, warding off the kisses and, as best he could, looking each one in the eye. "See you next year, James," one of them said. "Take good care of Gran."

On they came, one after another, every shape and size, Peckham after Peckham. As the boy stood there pumping each hand that came along, with the steady hum of the dynamos in his ears, scraps of the band music and the speeches of the afternoon floated through his head. "It is altogether fitting and proper that we should do this," a piping voice kept saying as the file moved past him. "Altogether fitting . . . altogether proper . . . not in vain."

James's room had been given over to upstate cousins, and he was sleeping in the attic alone. He didn't care for it much. In the months since he had come to live with Gran, he had spent many hours there, until the attic had become for him a

dark cavern with many grottoes, each of them peopled with its
own set of ghosts. By the stairwell was a crib, now folded up and
put away, in which he had slept the one time his mother and
father had brought him to visit there. It was almost the earliest
thing he could remember. In one of the alcoves made by the
dormer windows was a leather trunk he had been told not to
open. He had gone through it once; everything in it was much
older than he—faded brown snapshots, keys powdering into
rust, sea shells, tasseled dance programs, plaited rings of hair.
Behind him, in another alcove, were things from home, books
and dishes and silver, packed up in New York early that spring.
The raw-wood smell of the boxes and barrels was still fresh.

He switched off the bare overhead light and crawled into the
bed that had been made up for him near the windows looking
west toward the lake. It was still hot and muggy. The rain, which
he could hear lightly falling upon the roof above him, had not
really cooled the attic off at all, but he was cold under the mil-
dewed covers. His ankles were sore where they had pressed
against the legs of the chair during the fireworks. So was his
right arm; it seemed as though he had not stopped shaking
hands. "Goodbye, James. Goodbye until next year," the voices
kept saying. "Take good care of Gran." He felt more tired than
he had the first night he came to the house to stay, when the
joggle and clack of the train had gone on and on in his head.
Now it was the fireworks he saw, blossoming slowly, slowly,
more slowly by far than he had seen them, with their explosions
muffled and remote. He lay on his back with his eyes closed and
watched them, listening to the steady rain and waiting for sleep.

He was also waiting, as he waited every night, for the crash
of the plane, but tonight it did not come. The breeze, freshening,
brought with it the smell of the pines in the yard, and soon he
was aware of nothing outside himself but the pines and the rain.
The odor of pines flowed over him. Gradually, the colored lights
that filled his brain grew smaller and smaller, and in his head

now was a Christmas tree, its flaming ornaments the artificial fires of the night. It was last Christmas's tree. He could see it and smell it. Last Christmas, when he and his mother and father had taken all morning just to open the presents, when watches and bright silk scarves and jeweled bracelets hung from the branches of the tree, and he had taken his new bicycle out to ride in Central Park through a lightly drifting snow. Suddenly, James saw his mother and father clearly, tousled and laughing, just as they looked that morning. He was astonished at the recollection. For the first time he was able to remember his parents without pain. He held the picture in his mind as long as he could, savoring it.

And now he lay wide awake in his bed again and listened to the rain falling steadily upon the roof above his head. Strength was coming back to him from some source he did not understand, and the aches in his muscles were no longer there. It's settling down to an all-night rain, he thought, and tomorrow the perch should be biting. In the morning, if it clears up a little, I'll get up early while Gran is still asleep and go down to the pier to catch a string of perch for breakfast. She'll be tired tomorrow, he said to himself. She'll sleep late. I'll be back before she knows I'm gone.

One of
the Famous Days

Leo Whitman considers himself a sensitive, sober man, but from time to time he has run with a drinking crowd and been drawn to loud women. He lived with Madeline Thompson for two years, off and on, and left her finally one day in late spring, walking out of her apartment on Central Park West leaving behind half his clothes and whatever else of his was there, because in the depth of his being he could no longer stand the life. The booze and the parties, their raffish friends, Madeline's scenes, their Sunday night fights that would end with his striking her against his will. Leo wanted to be by himself. He went back to his own apartment in the Village; he mailed Madeline the keys to her place; he had his phone disconnected; he began to keep a journal; he changed jobs, from one trade publication to another; he read a lot; he studied Vedanta; he went off the sauce. His senses began to awaken. He began to feel like a man. "I have truly forgotten how to look at things," he said to himself. He began to look around him as hard as he could and walked through the city, to and from work, through Central Park on summer evenings and winter Sundays, looking, looking. He found he could almost get along without women. Was it the concentration exercises or was he getting older? For most of the summer, fall, and winter he went without alcohol, society, or sex.

Then it was May and then June. On a day when the sign on the Newsweek building read 93°, not long after the noon sirens had sounded, Leo stood, looking, waiting to cross Fifth Avenue at the corner of Forty-ninth Street, and saw in front of Saks's curved corner window, where she was waiting (he supposed) for her lover, a light-haired girl in a short yellow dress and a broad-brimmed white straw hat. Her arms and legs were pale and absolutely bare. As Leo looked at her, the breeze that flows on Forty-ninth Street quickened and she raised one hand to hold her hat. Something in her gesture made him think of the way Madeline had looked when she was at her prettiest, in the snapshots she had shown him from her Wellesley days. The light changed to green and Leo crossed Fifth Avenue, but he could not catch his breath; desire for that girl possessed him. And then her image went out of his head, leaving a dry lust behind, for the breeze became a wind and blew dirt into his left eye.

Leo had taught himself to suffer pain and attacks of anxiety quietly. By exhaling deeply, by repeating the prayers he had been given by the Swami—*Om Tat Sat* and *Tat tvam asi* and the one he liked best, the one he used in packed elevators and halted subway trains, "Let all beings be happy; let all beings be peaceful; let all beings be blissful."—he was able to endure traffic delays, the dentist's drill, and the last hour of business lunches without flinching or breaking for the door. But lesser discomforts still set him on edge. As he walked through Rockefeller Center in the hot air past the plantings of roses, holding down the lid of his eye, making his way among camera-hung tourists and bare-throated office girls in the noontime sun, anger welled up in him to keep company with his lust. He was hungry, the thing in his eye was not to be washed away by forced tears, and the burden of the city seemed more than he could bear. He had planned to be back in his office on Second Avenue with a sandwich and a container of milk by one, but he kept on going west away from work, half blind, bumped and jostled, running from the alien crowds.

He turned north on Sixth Avenue and then after a few blocks he turned west again, until he saw that he had fallen into one of his old beaten paths, the one that led to Fan's place, their old bar, Madeline's and his. He had not been there since the breakup, not for more than a year, and now there was nowhere else he could think of to go. For blocks he had been fighting his way through the acrid air, the sun hot on his head. Fan's would be cool, and though there was the good chance he would run into Madeline, at least he was sure to be welcomed and sure to see someone he knew.

Fan's is an ordinary place, a long bar with a row of booths and behind it a dining room with a dozen or so tables. For the regulars, it's like a high-school hangout. Most of them are in show business or have been, and they go to Fan's to restate their claim to youth and their immunity to time; it shows in their eyes and in the laughter. Fan's drinks are large and the food simple. Both are expensive, but not everyone pays. Fan, who was once in show business herself, has been running the place for years, since her husband died, and, as she says, she tries to take care of her own.

When Leo first started seeing Madeline, she had a steady job at a television studio a few blocks away, and although it was more than Leo could afford and a long trip crosstown for him besides, they would have lunch at Fan's on payday and drinks there once or twice a week. Fan liked them, Madeline especially, and sometimes she would pick up their tab. When Leo left Madeline, he left Fan's too, along with every place he and Madeline had gone to. He never wanted to see her again. He was like that. He knew that Madeline still hung out at Fan's, and until today it was almost the last place in the world that he wanted to go.

Leo walked into Fan's, pulling the door shut behind him to keep out the city air. It was quiet inside; Fan's has no times or seasons, only perpetual cool pink twilight. Leo stood at the door for a moment patting his forehead dry with a wad of Kleenex. Nothing at all was changed. Above the bar were the Christmas decorations that had always hung there. Along the bar were familiar shapes, and at the far end he saw John, the day bartender, a dim white oval in the dusk. The thing in Leo's eye itched cruelly and he still could not catch his breath. He ran the gauntlet of the bar—they all turned to greet him. "Hi, Marv. Hi, Milt. Hi, Sam. Hi, Louise, how've you been?" he said—and took a stool near the end. John was muddling an old-fashioned and frowning; he disapproved of fancy drinks. He glanced up at Leo over the edge of rimless eyeglasses. "You're looking well, Mr. Whitman," he said. He wiped his hands and stuck one out over the bar. Leo shook it. "How are you, John?" he said, more heartily than he had expected. "Not bad for an old man," John said. He moved down the bar with the old-fashioned, as easily as if he were on electric roller skates.

When John came back, Leo said, "I have this thing in my damn eye." "Try holding the lid down, Mr. Whitman," John said. Leo held the lid down again and asked for a ginger ale and a menu. If Fan's steak sandwich hadn't gone up over four fifty, he would have one at the bar. When he heard Madeline's voice behind him, he was only a little surprised. It was early for her, though. Had she reformed? The last months he had been living with her, she rarely surfaced before three. He looked up to see her reflection in the mirror above the back bar just as she caught sight of him. "Oh, Christ. Leo," she said. Leo let his eyelid go and stared at her reflection. "Look who's here, Mrs.

Thompson," John said. Leo turned around, got off the stool, and kissed Madeline on the cheek. "Hello, Madeline," he said. "Hello, Leo," she said, and then she said "*John,*" and leaned over the bar as she always did—John bent to meet her—and kissed John's cheek. Then she sat down on the stool next to Leo. "Oh God, don't look at me, I just got up," she said, and turned toward her reflection above the bottles, smoothing the hair along her temples with the heels of her hands. Damp blond hairs strayed about her neck and behind her ear. She had aged less than Leo expected. The white linen dress she wore was one he remembered. Her arms were bare, too, but thicker than the girl's on the corner. She asked John for a glass of ice water and drank it down, then turned toward Leo, crossing her legs. Their knees touched and Leo desired her. They might have just met. "How do I look to you, Leo?" she said.

A bit of hair had fallen across her forehead and Leo touched it back into place with a finger. "You look good," he said. "You look just the same."

"I still drink," she said. "I'm a tiny bit drunk right now if you really want to know." John brought her a second glass; it was heavy-bottomed and held, so far as Leo could tell, at least a double Gibson. He counted five onions. "John always gives it to me in this glass. He doesn't trust me," Madeline said. She laughed. "*You* know. 'Anything lighter at this hour of the morning would fly out of my hand like a frightened dove.'" This was one of the famous lines, Leo remembered, first delivered—where was it?—at the old Moriarty's or Costello's or P. J. Clarke's when the old man was still alive by—who was it? —Peter Hall or Andy Colangelo or . . . it was Fred Oates. Fred, an old admirer of Madeline's, had been buried from Frank E. Campbell's the spring before; it was one of the last times Leo had gone out in public with Madeline and the last time he had seen the group together. By now, the day Fred was buried would have become one of the famous days. There were famous lines, famous jokes, famous days. Madeline memorialized them all.

Madeline bent to sip from the glass on the bar, then lifted it nearly to the level of her chin. "First today," she said as she always did, and looked at Leo over the glass. He raised his glass of ginger ale. She seemed pleased to see him.

"What in *hell* are you drinking?" she said. Leo told her. He no longer really needed booze, he said. He'd lost his taste for it, and for cigarettes.

"Don't you ever get *thirsty?*" Madeline asked him.

Leo didn't want to sound stuffy. Between them, he and Madeline had drunk at least a quart of gin a day, and they would be well into a second by the end of Saturday night. He'd developed a liking for wines, he told her, and Danish beer, and Campari and soda before dinner. His senses were more alive now. He'd get cravings for odd things. Things he'd drunk when he was a kid—cherry phosphates, Green Rivers, ammonia Cokes. Or a huge ice-cold navel orange, or coconut milk, or a nice piece of Cranshaw melon. Right now, he'd like a piece of Cranshaw melon.

"Don't you ever want to just *drink?*" Madeline said.

Leo said no, he honestly didn't think so.

"Are you happy?" she asked. "You were always saying you wanted to be happy."

On the whole, he was, Leo said. In little things, anyway. He would be happy right now if he didn't have something in his goddam eye.

Madeline was immediately attentive. "Which eye is it?" she said. Leo pointed. "Oh, *sweetie*, it's all red," she said. "We'll take that out right now." She swung on her stool to face Leo head on and took his chin in her hand. "Look at Mommie," she said, and lifted up the eyelid. Leo shivered again, and remembered Madeline naked. In the summer in her apartment when they were alone she was nearly always naked. There were no air conditioners. She would walk in the door zipping off her dress and cry, "Christ, Leo! It's *hot*. Fix us a drink."

"Damn," Madeline said. "Get off the stool. You're too high. In this light I can't see a thing." A piece of hair had again slipped down upon her forehead and quivered in the breeze from the air conditioner behind them. It was peaceful here. Sinatra was on the juke. Sinatra. They would dance to old Sinatras— "I've GOT you under my skin."—and then make love. "Get off the stool, Leo," Madeline said.

John rummaged around the back bar until he found a flashlight. Leo stood, knees bent, before Madeline. John turned the light on Leo's eye and Madeline, with the corner of the handkerchief she pulled from Leo's breast pocket, flicked out the piece of dirt. She poked the handkerchief back into the pocket and kissed Leo's eyebrow. "There, there. All better now," she said.

Leo straightened up slowly and sat down on his stool. Though the thing seemed to be in his eye still, he supposed it was gone. "I'm hungry," he said to Madeline. "Let me buy you lunch." She nodded, her mind somewhere else. "Get us a booth," she said. "I'll be right *avec*." Leo watched her walk away through the back room. He had forgotten how small she was. She rolled when she walked, tottering slightly on the unstylish high heels she always wore, as if she suspected that the floor might suddenly pitch beneath her. Nothing held her together but thin wires and will, Leo thought. He wondered how she was getting on without him.

Leo called his office to say he wouldn't be back much before three, took a booth near the bar—the place was still half empty —and sat waiting for Madeline to come back, a fresh ginger ale before him and a fresh Gibson for her. His anger was gone, the itch was gone, he could breathe. He watched the bubbles in his ginger ale rise to the surface and pop as they reached the air.

When he was a child and feverish his mother always gave him ginger ale and the bubbles stung his nose. Now when he put his nose down to the glass and sniffed he could barely feel their sting. Life was shorter than he had expected. Was he happy? The truth was that he was becoming a solitary monster. His life had gone flat. Should he have a drink, then? He didn't think so. No. He was wary of Madeline. She stirred his blood.

Madeline was a long time returning. She had stopped to talk with Fan, she said, who was back there with a couple of her cronies. Leo would have to stop by, too, and say hello. When the waiter came, Madeline sent her glass back for more ice and more gin and Leo ordered two steak sandwiches, rare. They were five dollars now.

"Aren't you sore at me?" he said.

"You could have called me," she said. "I'm not anathema or anything, am I?"

"You said they always call back. I was going to be the one who didn't," Leo said. "And I cut off my phone."

"I know."

"I wanted to be by myself."

"No girls?"

"Village girls. Girls at the office. Nothing serious. Hardly any. How's Sandy?" Sandy was Madeline's best friend.

"The same. She thinks she may be getting married."

"How's Peter?" Peter Hall was another old friend, a former beau.

"Peter will never change. Why do you think I'm here at this ungodly hour? You sure you wouldn't like a drink?"

The steak sandwiches came and they ate for a while. "Tell me about Peter," Leo said.

"Oh, that," Madeline said, still eating, and wiped her mouth with her napkin. She sipped her drink. "We saw him off at Kennedy last night. He's gone to the Coast for a month. Sandy and I saw him off."

"Tell me."

"Well. *Typ*ical. The takeoff was late, *as* usual, and we'd gone out there early anyhow so we could all have dinner together before Peter left—you know he can't bear to get on a plane sober or alone. We went out in a Carey Cad—air conditioned, my dear—with a thermos of martinis, so you can imagine. And after dinner, such as it was, we sat around the London Bar under those green pool-hall lights drinking eighty-five brandies and staring at that departures board on the TV set above the bar, with Peter getting sadder and sadder, poor baby. He really hates to fly. He sat there getting *green* with those red-rimmed eyes brimming over, and trying hard to smile, which made him look like an archaic Greek. Then she called the plane and we walked him down that red and white tunnel, re-*verb*erating from side to side, and right onto the plane. Then Sandy and I had to take the damn bus back—no cabs, no cabs, and we'd let Peter send the Cad away, which is where we made our big mistake—and we fell asleep on the bus, *naturellement*, and woke up in the East Side Terminal with the most godawful headaches and thirsts. So we came over to Fan's. Sam and Milt were here, and Dave of course, and Edie Oates, who's been a lot more fun since Fred died, I must say, and when Fan closed the place we went up to *my* place and played records. *Tosca*, I think. And then Fan says I threw everybody out, even Sandy. Anyway, there was nobody there this morning."

Leo had heard a hundred such stories and been through a hundred such nights. He knew what most of them were really like. But then didn't she? How could she go on believing that those times were fresh and new?

Madeline sipped her drink. "Well, when I woke up this morning—thank God I *was* alone, these days you never know—At least with you I felt safe. So to speak." She giggled. "I mean, you kept me from the *rest*, at least." She looked at Leo, her head cocked coyly, one hand splayed upon her chest. "When I woke up this morning, I was *parched*," she said. "You do remember what that was like, I suppose?"

"I would make us brown cows," Leo said.

"God, was I *thirsty* this morning. Not for booze. For anything, *anything* cold and wet. You know how hot it's been. So. . . . I turn on the tap in the bathroom. No water. Can you believe it? They'd turned the water off. So, out of bed I go (naked, thought Leo) and down the hall to the kitchen. Try the tap there. Nothing. Three drops. Open the fridge. Nothing. Not A Thing. Those bastards last night didn't leave a thing. They cleaned me out. No juice, no Coke, no milk. Not even any ice. Nothing in the box but a half bottle of Pinot Blanc from God knows when. It was probably there when you left me. So I drank the stuff. Glug."

"And?"

"All I felt was worse. Then naturally I couldn't sleep, so I got dressed and came down here. There was no water and I couldn't shower. I didn't do anything to my hair. Am I talking too much?"

"Finish your steak," Leo said.

"I've had all I want. I told Fan you're dying for a nice piece of Cranshaw melon and she says you're months too soon. I said you've developed peculiar tastes since we saw you last. She wants you to come back and say hello. You don't have to be nice to me but you ought to be nice to Fan."

Leo went back after a while and was nice. A couple of actors he vaguely recognized were with Fan eating lunch. When he got back to the booth, Madeline had a new drink. Leo decided to have one too; he was not a moralist, after all, and he had never enjoyed being cold sober while Madeline was around. He asked for a Gibson, and John brought it himself. It was a double, and on the house. "Nice to have you back, Mr. Whitman," John said. Leo clinked glasses with Madeline and said sadly, "Here's to crime."

Madeline said, "I have every reason in the world to hate you, Leo, and I can't."

"I miss everything but the fights," Leo said. "Sometimes I miss the fights."

Madeline nodded, or Leo thought she did, and he took her hand. He had missed her like hell, he said, but he couldn't stand the pace. Besides, he had to graduate from kindergarten *some-day*, he said.

"Has it never occurred to you that kindergarten is all it all is?" Madeline said.

"I had to get out," Leo said.

"You're funny. I don't think you're normal," Madeline said. "What's it done for you? You can't even hold on to a girl. I thought you'd go right out and grab yourself one of those nice round nineteen-year-olds."

"I tried," Leo said. "I didn't know what to say to them. I took one to the Electric Circus and she laughed at me. 'You're as bad as my mother and father,' she said. 'You're doing the *twist*.' She was interesting in bed, but we had nothing to say."

"So," Madeline said, her eyes clouded. "So." She was getting stoned, all right, Leo thought. This was how their fights always went. She would prod him to tell her about other girls, then turn on him in rage and provoke him with names. Then he would strike her. Then he would put her to bed.

"You can't be enjoying this," Leo said.

"Do you have any idea what you did to me leaving like that?" she said. "Do you have any idea what you did to yourself?"

"I thought this would happen if I saw you," Leo said.

"I could have had my revenge—you don't *know*—but what the hell . . . Now I'm just sorry for you, you poor creep. Excuse me." She got up again.

It was the moment for Leo to go, but he stayed. "I *thought* you'd still be sore," he said to Madeline when she came back.

Her mood had changed again. She fished an onion out of her glass and sucked it. "Oh, I forgive you," she said. "Why the hell not? But you were a fool to leave. Don't you know I gave you a home? That was your *home,* sweetie."

"It got so I was afraid of you," Leo said.

"Afraid of me?"

"That's the truth. We started having all those fights. I was getting afraid of you."

"Afraid? You, of all people, afraid of *me?*" Madeline's eyes clouded again. "I loved you," she said.

They sat there looking at each other. Then the light came back into Madeline's eyes. "Oh, *pardon.* I forgot something," she said, rising. "I'll be right right back. Don't move."

Leo watched her walk away, weaving now as if she had just stepped ashore from a boat that had been rocking for hours in a choppy sea. He could see her cross the back room, stopping to say something to someone, and then he saw her go through the kitchen service door. Something was in store for him, he supposed—one of Fan's famous surprises. The place was crowded now, and Leo saw more faces that he knew or thought he knew. Was he drunk on one drink? He saluted all the familiar faces with a wave of his hand. A few people waved back, and Sam Conlon, who had been at the bar since Leo came in, walked over to say hello. Then Leo saw Madeline coming toward him. She was carrying something large in both hands and walking toward him straight and slow, like a bride. People were staring. The buzz and gabble hushed. Faces blossomed, white and tanned and pink, as everyone turned toward him. Leo felt he had super-sight. He knew them all.

What Madeline carried in her arms, he could now see, was a Georgia watermelon, almost round, pale green, larger than a basketball, with a yellow ribbon tied around it and bunched at the top in a lopsided bow. Madeline held the thing as if it were alive and ready to spring out of her hands and skitter off through the bar like a green greased pig. Leo saw her frown in concentration and then smile, stretching out her arms toward him. She was almost upon him. He braced himself, involuntarily, and his legs stuck out suddenly into her path. She veered and teetered for a moment before she got her balance. But now the melon began to elude her. She had meant to present him with the melon, Leo saw. This was no act of revenge. She had been cradling it in her arms as if it were a newborn child. If we had ever had a child, would it look like that? he thought. Unable to hold either herself or the melon up any longer, Madeline flung her arms wide and collapsed at Leo's feet. The watermelon exploded on the table, spraying them both with juice and pale pink watery meat. Madeline hid her face in her hands, laughing. "Oh dear oh dear oh dear," she said. "Oh, Leo, I'm so sorry. We made it just for you. Dear Leo. It was absolutely *plein du rhum.*"

Leo laughed, too, and his eyes teared from that and the rum fumes until he could barely see. Sam Conlon came over and helped Madeline to her feet. Fan came over with her actors, and Milt, and Edie Oates, and just then Sandy came in with Tom, her fiancé. They had had lunch at Downey's and were just stopping in for a Stinger on their way back to work. They never got back. Neither did Leo. How could he, soaked in watermelon juice and rum? Madeline took him to her place and they changed—his clothes were still hanging in a closet— and the rest of the group came up later. That turned into one of the most famous days of all—more than a *day*. It went on for three days and three nights. Leo and Madeline stayed together for a few months after that, but it didn't last. Now Leo is off the sauce again, and he has his inner life back, and he knows some new prayers, and he is looking around him at the world much as before. But Leo is still remembered at Fan's.

Cape Trip

few months before they decided to get married, Eric Pearce rented a car and drove up to Cape Cod with Sally Rowland for the long New Year weekend. He had been seeing Sally since that October and had been asking her to go away with him practically since they met, but this was the first time she had said yes. She didn't understand why he insisted so. After all, they saw each other all the time. Weekends didn't mean too much to her; she wanted to get out of New York for good. But Eric wanted to take her away from the city, to see how they would get along traveling together. He was thinking of marrying her, though it was too soon to tell her that. When she finally agreed to go with him, he didn't know where to go, and only decided on the Cape because they would be away from the ski crowds there and they would be sure, at least, to find plenty of sea and sky.

How they loathed New York! The place was really too much for them, and it was so hard to break its spell. In the autumn, they had bicycled in the park and gone for long walks and seen all the movies there were, but now that it was cold they seemed to spend their Saturdays and Sundays in bed—in Eric's apartment on West Tenth Street or in Sally's uptown when her roommate was away. They liked to make love, but they weren't always making love. Much of the time they were sitting around, too tired or too lazy to move, watching the tube or with the Sunday *Times* on their laps. Or playing gin. The city was wearing them down. They had to get out for good. But how? They had both been in Europe and been happy there. They had had their *Wanderjahre,* Sally for two long summers in Spain and Italy and Greece, and Eric (after he had taken his Army discharge in Frankfurt) bumming his way around the Mediterranean for more than two years, and as far east as Baghdad. Now they were (supposedly) settling down, into their New York careers. Eric was a copywriter at what seemed to him a fantastic salary in one of the clever advertising agencies—though he refused to think of himself as an ad man, or as clever. Sally was already on the masthead of one of the teenage fashion magazines. But they wanted to go back to Europe, to the Mediterranean. They had begun to learn how to live simply there. The city was too complex; it was corrupting them; it cost too much. They talked of living on Crete or Samos or near Tunis somewhere. They longed for the Mediterranean sun, to be really warm in that way again. In Europe, they had felt free. Oh, to be unencumbered, without roots! "How *can* you be?" Eric, who was a little older, would say sometimes. "I mean, as a permanent thing? Can you be a bum forever?" But he wanted it, too.

"What kind of car would you like?" Eric asked Sally when he called her at her office Friday morning.

"Make it a red one," she said, in her jokey way.

"Most rented cars are red," he said. For all he knew, this was true.

They both had to work until nearly six, which gave them a late start in heavy traffic. The car was red and smelled new, but it didn't have much power. Going up FDR drive, Eric drove cautiously. Sally sat beside him in her fur-trimmed coat looking out at the traffic through yellow sunglasses. It was already dark. Cars in the outer lanes roared steadily by them.

"We're trapped in a herd of mad buffalo," Eric said. "Can you imagine commuting and doing this every night?"

"You'd get used to it," Sally said. She laughed. "I sound like my mother," she said. "She thinks you can get used to anything. In her view of life, a woman should. It's the Christian, long-suffering way."

"I *would* get used to it," Eric said. "That's the trouble. I got used to New York. I came here three years ago with my eyes and ears open and now most of the time they're shut. Who can stay open to all *this?*" His gesture encompassed the Sutton Place apartments above them, the hurtling cars, the East River and the Pepsi-Cola sign across the river, and Welfare Island, and the Fifty-ninth Street bridge. "How do people stand it?" he said.

"You know," Sally said. "You flip out now and then. Or you turn on. Or you drink."

"Or you get out sometimes. We never get out."

"Well," Sally said. "We are."

Eric held to the right-hand lane. "I'm driving like my father," he said.

"I'm riding like my mother," Sally said. She was sitting erect, her hands on her lap, braking involuntarily now and then.

They were both still too young not to be consciously op-pressed by parental ghosts. Their parents wrote regularly and telephoned often, Sally's especially, which made it worse. The Pearces in Indianapolis and the Rowlands in Wilmington were much alike in some ways. They were large families and they believed in family. They expected children to grow up and marry and settle down and carry on the family in the old tradi-tion. Now? In times like these? To Eric and Sally, born in the forties, that life had begun to seem out of the question by their early teens. Though they weren't rebels, exactly. And they loved their parents; they didn't *want* to dissappoint them.

"My father taught me to drive," Eric said. "He always drives like this, both hands on the wheel in the ten-minutes-to-two position—seven miles over the limit in the country and three in the towns. Never an accident. Never a summons. He drove a thousand miles a week for years, visiting milk stations in Indiana."

"*Milk* stations? Why did he visit milk stations?"

"That was his job then. He was inspector for the Indianapolis milk shed."

"Oh," Sally said. "I thought it might be his hobby. My grandfather, Grandpa Rowland, used to go to Paris every year to visit the Cathedral of Notre Dame, and his office was full of books about it and pictures of the gargoyles. When I was little I had the feeling he was very religious; his office was like a shrine. We all thought he was an expert on Notre Dame, and then it turned out he was crazy. Mother still calls it his hobby."

"My father isn't crazy," Eric said. Sally's family had money; his didn't. Sally's family was full of eccentrics; his people were dull. He didn't like to be reminded of these things.

"I don't think my grandfather was crazy either," Sally said. "But they had him put away. Mother is always saying brightly, 'Everyone needs a hobby. Father has his golf and Grandfather has his Notre Dame.' She said it the last time I was in Wilmington, and he's been in the hospital for five years."

How little they knew of each other's past, Eric thought. He had never heard of her grandfather; she had no idea of what his father did. But that was part of living for the moment, which was how they tried to live. To live in their senses, to look with both eyes. It was what he had done when he was hitching around the Mediterranean, or had been learning to do.

"Right or left?" Eric said to Sally. He trusted her sense of direction and not his own. He had forgotten to look at a map.

Right led through the Bronx and left through Harlem. "I think we have to go through the Bronx," Sally said. Before long they were on the turnpike, the radio was playing rock, and Sally was sitting close to him holding his hand. After a while she said, "I'm sleepy. I'm going to put my head in your lap and take a nap." She took off her coat, lay down with the coat over her and her head just fitting between Eric and the wheel, and slept. Eric turned off the radio. The first time they came to a toll station, she sat up, but after that she slept. Eric touched her cheek and hair and breast now and then and thought how pretty she was in that well-bred Eastern way, with her long rust-colored hair and her snub nose and fair freckled skin—she didn't tan well; her suit marks barely showed—and flecked green-gray eyes. She was nearly as tall as he. They fit well. She laughed a lot. Whenever she was angry with him she would hit him lightly in the chest with her fist. It was better than harboring things, she said. But she never argued and she bore no grudges. Though she showed a dark side sometimes in her fretfulness and her dreams, and in that jokey brightness. He could tell when she was being too bright. And she always excited him. The weight of her head right now, warm on his lap, excited him, aroused him. Thinking of traveling with her as man and wife—he had bought her a wedding ring for the trip—aroused him.

When Sally woke she said, "I usually don't do that. You see how I trust you. Putting my head in your lap and not being afraid."

"You slept like a child," Eric said.

"I could never do that with my father."

"No one ever did that with me before," Eric said.

"I guess it was my cold," Sally said when she finally sat up. She had had her usual Christmas cold, but it was almost over. She began to brush her hair. "I love sleeping in cars," she said. "I miss cars in New York."

"At home, we were in cars two or three hours a day," Eric said.

"At *least*. I'd love to have my own car again."

"We used to have a place in the Indiana dunes where we went for weekends and summer vacations," Eric said. "It was a long drive home and when I was little they would put me on the back seat to sleep alone. Just before we got home, at the last long hill before the house, my father and mother would wake me and I'd stand on the seat and watch the car's shadow as we went under the overhead lights. The shadow would be long and thin and faint behind us and then get shorter and darker and *thicker*, somehow, until it disappeared under the car just as if it had been sucked up by a giant vacuum cleaner. My father thought I liked to watch it, and he would turn off the ignition and coast home very slowly, and I would have to watch our shadow be sucked up and disappear over and over again. Something about it made me dizzy and almost sick to my stomach. It frightened me, but I couldn't stop watching. They didn't mean to be cruel—they never do—and it was nothing I could *explain*. But it was such a long hill. Everything is so much longer and larger when you're a child, like a high."

"Eternal recurrence," Sally said. "That's Nietzsche." She'd had a tutorial in philosophy her junior and senior years and she would say these things. *"The eternal recurrence even of the smallest—that was my disgust with all existence—Nausea! Nausea!* It made him sick, too."

"This wasn't so eternal," Eric said. "The Interstate comes through there now. The old road is gone. The *hill* is gone, and sodium lights don't cast a shadow. It's too bad. I miss that hill."

"Don't look back," Sally said. This was one of their rules; Sally liked to make rules. They were not to talk much of the past, and if they did it was to be without nostalgia. They were not to talk of their jobs. They were to live in the moment and with their senses. It was the way to joy. The city, ridden with plagues, was their enemy, and so was America, the complacent middle-class America they had been brought up in without their

consent. They weren't escapists. They were looking for something more real, more pure, than anything their parents knew.
Eric agreed with her, or thought he did, though he wouldn't
have put everything in quite the same way.

They stopped for the night in a floodlit colonial motel on
the outskirts of New Haven, just off the turnpike. Eric parked
fifty yards away from the office entrance, and Sally, who was
shyer than he had expected her to be, waited in the car while he
checked in. Snow half filled the swimming pool and was
heaped against the motel's red brick walls, but their room was
warm and smelled of sandalwood. Painted cherry blossoms
bloomed on the gold wallpaper above a low orange bed. Swing-
ing shoji-screen doors, one of them slightly ajar, led to a dressing room with a mirrored wall. Eric brought in the bags while
Sally went down the hall for ice. She was gone for what seemed
to him a long time. When she came back, she put a cold hand
on his cheek. "I hope you appreciate what I've done for you,"
she said. "There was no ice ready in the machine, and the cubes
were dropping slowly, slowly, like starving snails from the side
of their cage. I caught each one as it fell in my hand." Slowly,
slowly like the shadows of the car from the back window, Eric
thought. He had almost the same eerie feeling now he had had
then. Something was happening to his sense of time. He took
a bottle of Ricard (*"le vrai pastis de Marseilles"*) from his
canvas carryall and made drinks, golden yellow and tasting of
anise. "It's like drinking sunlight," Sally said. "On the Riviera,
we always drank it in the afternoon."

The restaurant next door to the motel was crowded, and
they waited to be called to a table in a large, dim cocktail lounge
that was nearly empty. Everything in the lounge was blue-green
except the pink and yellow plastic flowers in vases on the walls
and the goldfish in the aquarium above the bar. Sally and Eric

sat on a banquette in the submarine light and ordered vodka on the rocks.

"This could be Indianapolis," Eric said. "Or Milwaukee or Louisville or Detroit. I never expected this of New Haven. But once you're out of Manhattan you could be any place in the States, I guess. I suppose that's why we're all in Manhattan."

"I met a man from Atlanta on Crete who hadn't been home for years," Sally said. "He was nice. He told me he'd always felt like an alien at home, and it was better to go someplace where you really were alien, because then it was a natural thing."

"He sounds like a twenties expatriate," Eric said.

"What's wrong with that? He was old enough. I wish I'd been old enough. I'm a throwback, I think."

"We're less desperate than they were, though."

"Less? We're more. What do you think? Just because we have money. . . . Just because we don't talk about it. . . . They only thought they were desperate, and we *are*. But of course the whole world's been desperate since the Bomb, so our generation's despair may not be so noticeable."

She was probably right, Eric thought, but if she was right why were they so happy?

The restaurant was larger and brighter than Eric had expected. At the tables were noisy family parties and parties of friends and a few couples who also seemed to be in New Haven just for the night. Sally ordered crabmeat au gratin and Eric ordered fried Ipswich clams. A boy wearing a chef's hat stopped by with watermelon pickle and cottage cheese and popovers and corn bread. There were side dishes of eggplant and home-fried potatoes and green beans, and bowls of salad with Caesar dressing. They asked for a bottle of Graves.

"Who could eat all this?" Sally said. "It's worse than home. New York must have the only restaurants in the country where it's possible to clean your plate."

"These are just like Howard Johnson clams," Eric said. "I thought they'd be juicy inside like oysters. The Ipswich fooled me."

"I don't see why," Sally said. "Ipswich isn't juicy."

The snow crunched underfoot as they walked back to their room. Icicles hung from the Old English motel sign. They put on nightshirts and played gin on the bed. Sally lost. "I think I can be feminine with you," she said to Eric. "The only other man I've been able to lose to with pleasure was my first love, in college, when I was eighteen."

"No nostalgia," Eric said.

"Oh, no," Sally said. "That's over. None."

The room seemed even warmer now and the bed was soft, and although they thought they were tired they found themselves making love upon the orange spread. Eric took off Sally's nightshirt and his own. Sally was wearing the gold necklace he had given her for Christmas and the wedding ring. Something about that Chinese modern room, about being in a different bed, where hundreds of couples like those they had seen in the dining room must have been, excited him in an odd way. It seemed to excite Sally, too. She began slipping from the bed, off the side of the bed onto the floor, as he made love to her, first her long red hair and then her head touching the sand-colored carpet. Desert sands. How full and long her throat was with that gold against it! Eric came suddenly, and shivered. She had stirred him in the way the nude photographs in magazines had done once—still did. That troubled him. Not for moral reasons, he thought, but because what happened was not in his body so much as in his head and left him feeling jittery and incomplete. Because he had let the media, with their stock sex shots, get to him. He began to make love to Sally again. They were lying on their sides now, moving slowly, gazing at each other.

"We're not here," he said. "We're off in the woods somewhere. Deep in the woods." This was one of their incantations.

"We're in the charmed circle," Sally said. "We're lying in the sun. It's warm."

"I smell roses."

"Oh, that's nice. Roses in winter."

They were together now and before long they fell into deep sleep, but they woke before morning. The blankets had slipped to the floor and they were both cold. They had to get up and re-make the bed and then they could not get back to sleep. Their bodies were clammy and unpleasant to touch. They lay without touching for a long time.

"We have to get out of New York for good," Eric said. "Or it won't last."

"We have to get out," Sally said. "Or I'll turn into a New York bitch."

The thought was ridiculous to Eric, and he laughed. "You're not serious," he said, turning to her.

"No," she said. "In New York, 'bitch' isn't a meaningful category. Am I supposed to be serious?"

"Only lightly serious."

"The thing is to be seriously light."

They were beginning to feel warm again. Erie started to sing, softly,

> *New York can do things*
> *Your mother wouldn't understand.*
> *It can make a man out of a woman*
> *And a woman out of a man.*

He stopped; he couldn't carry a tune. "It's a Wilson Pickett blues," he said.

"Stop being serious," Sally said. "Cheer up. I know a blues that goes—

> *Here we sit like*
> *Birds in the wilderness*
> *Birds in the wilderness*
> *Birds in the wilderness.*

We used to sing it at camp when we were sitting at the table waiting to be fed." She sang it again.

"Shhhh," Eric said. "What's seriously light?"

"You know," Sally said. "The way we touch. The way we make love sometimes. The way it is when it's for the moment and we kiss the joy as it flies."

But why wasn't it easier? Eric thought. Making love was the best thing they had between them; it gave him almost his only sense, in the city, of really pure, intense life. And that kind of joy was so hard to hold on to. Tonight, no matter what they might say, they hadn't been close. He felt it. He was on edge, and she was edgy, too.

The motel served a free Continental breakfast in a sunny, drafty breakfast room. *"Croissants? Café au lait?"* Sally said as they entered. There was bottled o.j., coffee in paper cups, sticky buns, and sugared doughnuts. Sally had o.j. and black coffee and Eric had everything. They were wearing Levi's and heavy turtlenecks and peacoats now, and Sally had her fur hat and yellow sunglasses on. In the breakfast room with the sun flooding in over them it felt almost tropical.

"I had my horrible crocodile dream again," Sally said. "They're poison green in a dark brown river and they have great gaping toothy jaws and they start eating each other, very very slowly. I could smell the river. It was like a thousand Greek loos."

"What happens?" Eric said.

"Nothing. It's always the same. I stand on the bank for what feels like hours and watch them eat each other."

Eric's dream had been worse. But she has enough fears of her own, he thought. Why should I tell her mine?

They bought a quart of vodka and two canned martinis in a liquor store a few blocks from the motel. They had never seen canned martinis before. Eric asked the salesman the way back to the turnpike, and the man took him over to the front door and pointed it out, putting an arm around him.

"Does that bother you when somebody touches you like that?" Sally asked when they were back in the car.

"No," Eric said. "Not usually. People like me."

"I hate to be touched by strangers," Sally said.

"That's wasp, isn't it? Hating to be touched?" Eric said. "What did you do in Italy and Greece?"

"It's funny," Sally said. "I didn't mind. I don't mind when I'm with you. I'm someone else then. I was someone else there."

They needed Alka-Seltzer and aspirin and found a drugstore on the way to the turnpike in a neighborhood of weathered, condemned old buildings, their windows boarded over, and of empty lots strewn with rubble where other buildings had been. Above the waste rose great new uncompleted structures, shaped like silos, of gray poured concrete. Sally went into the drugstore while Eric waited in the car. She came back with her peacoat unbuttoned over the navy turtleneck and her fur hat askew. Eric opened the door for her. "God, you look eccentric," he said.

"Why did you say I looked eccentric?" Sally said when they were back on the turnpike. Her voice was sharp.

"We're both eccentric, aren't we?" Eric said. "It's a good word."

"You didn't say I *was* eccentric. You said I *looked* eccentric. That's no compliment."

"I thought it was. You look great."

"I'm hostile this morning," Sally said. "It's not you. I woke up cold again because you slept on the inside and left me near the window."

"Why didn't you tell me? I don't mind the outside."

"Oh, well," Sally said. "I'm not so hostile now. I really like you a lot."

It occurred to Eric that it was too soon to be certain that Sally loved him at all.

They stopped for lunch at a Howard Johnson's near the Mystic turnoff, though it was still early. They felt starved. The air now seemed almost warm, and they saw only a few patches of melting snow. They sat down in a booth by the window and a waitress came up and said, "Hello! My name's Margaret." She wore a large button with her name on it, too. They had glasses of milk and rare hamburgers with cole slaw, which they piled along with relish and mustard and catsup and slices of onion and tomato on top of the hamburgers. They took ice cream cones back to the car. "God, I hate being nasty. I was hungry," Sally said.

Eric said, "*My miracle is that when I am hungry I eat and when I am thirsty I drink.* That's an old Zen saying."

Sally laughed. "My miracle is that when I am hungry you feed me," she said.

A sign on the approach road read SEAPORT and pointed away from the turnpike. They drove down that way. "It's a *reconstruction*," Sally said when they saw the port. Reconstructions offended her; anything synthetic did. There was an admission fee, and they didn't go in, but looked at the old ships and the tidy eighteenth-century buildings from behind a white rail fence. In the parking lot across the road they found a Japanese suicide torpedo, sixty-four feet long according to the sign in front of it, half-filled amidships with candy wrappers, soft-drink cans, and dirty Kleenex. America then and America now, Eric thought. He was slipping into what he called his transcendental mood; everything was starting to seem symbolic. The torpedo was from the Second World War, and the sign explained that successful operation would involve the instantaneous destruction of both torpedo and operator. "In New York, the odds are about the same," Eric said. They took each other's picture there.

Once they were back on the turnpike, Sally fell asleep again with her head on Eric's lap. She still had her cold. There was little traffic, and Eric drove with an empty mind, the way he had during the summers when he was in college. Where were they? They might be anywhere. The country they were driving through was like the Indiana dunes, and water felt near. It might be Lake Michigan. Not long after they entered Rhode Island he saw a sign reading CAPE COD POINTS and followed it, turning off onto a narrow highway that ran between snowy fields. By the time Sally woke up he felt thoroughly lost; they were driving along a parkway through a forest of miniature Christmas trees with no houses or cars in sight.

"Where are we?" Sally said. "It's magical."

"I don't have any idea," Eric said.

"Oh, good."

"We're way off the main road. There were signs for a while saying this was the shortest way to the Cape, but the only sign I've seen lately said Jamestown. Isn't that in Virginia?"

"It doesn't matter," Sally said. "This is lovely. We don't have to be anyplace."

"We're not far from the water," Eric said. "I was beginning to miss you. You slept a long time."

They followed blue-and-white signs reading JAMESTOWN BRIDGE and after a while they crossed it, a long tollbridge over a broad sound. Gulls floated above them and below them in the hazy air. The sun was pale yellow. In Jamestown, large summer houses, their windows shuttered, looked blindly across the bay to Newport. More symbols, but of what? Eric thought. There was not a trace of snow. Tall towers stood in the bay, a single cable glinting between them. Before long, there would be a Newport Bridge, too. The approach to the nearest tower was about complete; a ramp rose up to it and stopped abruptly at the top. Beyond the tower a car ferry was leaving its slip. Eric drove up to the dock and parked beside a cream-colored XK-E. No one was in it. With the XK-E, they were first in line. They walked over to the ferry office. The next boat left in an hour, at three.

Beside the ferry building was a bar with a Schaeffer's sign in the window and men inside watching football on TV. "Perhaps we can have a Ricard or two while we're waiting," Sally said.

"Ricard?" Eric said. "Let's go down to the water first. They may not have Ricard here."

"All right," Sally said amiably. "We always found in France that a drink or two helps pass the time when there are these delays."

They walked down a street that led along the shore back of the ferry building. Water lapped against a gray stony beach. The pilings of a ruined pier extended into the water. They walked on down to the water and looked at Newport across the bay, where empty summer houses stared back at the empty Jamestown houses staring at them. The air felt like early spring. Eric pulled Sally to him and they kissed.

Gulls were perched on the old pilings. "Look at all the pigeons," Sally said.

"They're gulls," Eric said.

"Oh, that goes back to when we were unlearning names," Sally said. "Terry and I, my first summer abroad. Instead of all the names for birds, just pigeon. Instead of all the names for trees, just palm. We were on the Côte d'Azur at the time. Instead of all the names for dog, just dog. It was like thinking in new categories. It was a liberating thing."

There were times when she didn't make much sense, Eric thought. And who was Terry? A boy or a girl? He thought he wouldn't ask. "You should see all the pigeons with pretty tails in the Bronx Zoo," he said.

"You may need more names for birds in a sophisticated nomenclature," Sally said. "Maybe three. Pigeons on land, gulls at sea, and nightingales if they sing."

There were gulls in the air just above them. "The less you know the more you can see," Sally said. "Look at their feet. They use them to hold up their tails. I bet you never saw *that* before." Eric looked. He hadn't. The small pink feet stuck straight back like a diver's.

Close to the shore half a dozen small gulls paddled in circles, cheeping. "They think they're ducks," Eric said.

"They can't be," Sally said. "They're gulls. There are no ducks."

They walked back to the bar and had a beer. "I've been jumpy since we left," Eric said. "I don't know why. I guess it was wanting to be out of the city with you so much. But we're out now. We're traveling. This is how it would be."

"How what would be?"

"In Europe or wherever. How it would be together." It was another incantation, he thought. He was saying it, hoping to make it true.

"I'm jumpy, too," Sally said. "We're not quite out yet. It takes time."

There were two long lines of waiting cars by now, and men were walking up the lines collecting tolls. Eric and Sally ran back to the car, then paid the toll and sat waiting, the sun already low and directly in their eyes.

They were first on the ferry, in the front position with only an accordion gate between them and the water. Two deckhands chocked their front wheels. How splendid it was there! The bay was flat and the color of steel; they could see far up and down it. The sun, mild as its heat was, warmed them through the windows, and they took off their peacoats. Sally put her sunglasses on. "I feel like a star," she said.

Off to their left was the unfinished approach to the bridge, breaking off sharply a hundred feet above the water. Eric took his binoculars out of the carryall in the back seat and looked at it, then passed the binoculars to Sally. "I'll tell you something," he said. "I'm afraid of dying that way. Driving off an open bridge or pier and falling, falling, knowing you're going to die. It's *my* recurrent dream. I had it last night. I have the feeling it almost happened to me once, in a car sometime when I was very small."

"I know a woman who died like that," Sally said. "She was part Indian and very beautiful. Her husband found her somewhere in Mexico and married her when she was sixteen. Then he brought her back to Wilmington and taught her to speak good English—he told everybody she was Castilian—but she was always too subservient for him. She was a primitive, really. She had all the primitive virtues. He was in the contracting business and after the war he made a lot of money and had rich friends and she embarrassed him. When she was thirty-six and the children were practically grown—she must have been a wonderful mother—he told her he was going to divorce her. He wanted to marry someone else, someone he'd had an affair with for a long time, the wife of a friend. She got in their white Cadillac the next morning and drove down into Maryland and off a pier in one of those fishing towns, into Chesapeake Bay. I think of her sinking slowly down in that white Cadillac with its white leather seats—her long black hair floating, you know? Isn't that morbid and romantic? Her oldest daughter used to write me long letters that started off the way she always talked and then had awful things in them. 'My father is a monster. I want to kill him. I want to kill him.' Over and over again. Things like that. We were in school together."

"That happened in *Red Desert*," Eric said. "You thought Monica Vitti was going to drive off the pier in the fog. And of course Jeanne Moreau really did it in *Jules and Jim*." The idea of it gave him chills.

"It's the kind of thing that makes you think twice about marriage," Sally said.

The ferry's whistle blew once and they began to move across

the water. Eric and Sally looked at the opposite shore through the binoculars, watching its image, which seemed to Eric more intense than the reality, come slowly nearer. To the right was a house on an island. Both house and island were gray-green and appeared to be streaked with sea moss. The island seemed smaller than the house, and the house looked ready to fall into the bay. Sky showed through its corner windows. Eric's sense of unreality was growing painfully strong. On the far shore was a blockhouse, its gun ports facing them. The town was built upon a hill and its low buildings, rising up the slope, were pink, their outlines clear in the light of the low sun. "Provence," Sally said. "It's Provence." Tugs and fishing boats moved silently upon the water. The gulls overhead rode almost motionless before them. The ferry's vibration was gentle. They came to a single smooth wave from one of the fishing boats and met it, not feeling a thing.

"The world becomes a dream," Eric said.

"I'm floating, floating," Sally said.

They were first off the ferry, and Eric drove up the steep hill into town. "We could look at the houses," he said, thinking of the mansions they had seen from across the bay.

"Let's not sight-see," Sally said. "Let's go straight on."

But he missed a turn somewhere and they found themselves on a road leading past small vacation houses with neat lawns that were nearly green. The houses were painted in bright colors, blues and purples and pinks, and had chalk-white carpenter's Gothic trim.

A picture-book town. Unreal. . . . Nearly every car they met was driven by a blond boy or girl. Nearly every corner, it seemed, had a sign reading THE EPISCOPAL CHURCH WELCOMES YOU. . . .

"Your folks would love it here," Eric said. "So would mine. It's their kind of town."

They went back toward the business section, which looked

like any business section, and stopped for gas and directions. They were right on the road for the Cape, it turned out. They could never stay lost for long.

"I feel good," Eric said. He turned on a rock station.

"Me, too," said Sally. "That ferry. . . ."

"It was nice," Eric said. He could feel the reality coming back, and his spirits rise.

But it was past five o'clock by now and almost dark and they weren't even on the Cape. "The days are so short this time of year, especially when you start them at noon," Sally said. At last they came to a bridge and to Buzzard's Bay and the first Ho-Jo's they had seen for hours; they stopped there for coffee before going on down a broad, empty divided-lane highway. For miles there were no buildings and no lights, and then they came suddenly to a town that was larger and brighter than they expected. Here it was truly winter. Snow lay heavy on the ground. Mounds of it were banked high against the curbs and shone white and sparkling in the light from shop windows. Colored lights outlined houses and trees. A life-sized crèche stood on the town green. It was another picture-book place. But there was no one on the streets, and the few motels they saw were either deserted or shut.

Finally they passed what looked like a country club on the edge of town, where a fat boy in a red jacket stood before the entrance directing cars to parking places. It turned out to be an inn, and they were given a suite, two rooms in something called the Swiss Village, with knotty-pine walls and maple early-American furniture. The bedroom had twin beds, high and far apart. They pushed the beds together. "Our first real home," Sally said. "Though it's not quite the décor I would have chosen." Eric got ice from the bar in the main building and they opened the canned martinis and drank them on the rocks. The martinis were weak and heavy with vermouth. Then they changed clothes quickly, Eric into a checked jacket and white turtleneck and cords, Sally into a tan pants suit, and went to eat. They were starved again.

The restaurant was full and the cocktail lounge nearly full. Both were enormous. "No wonder the streets were empty," Eric said. The hostess took Eric's name and said, "Freddy will call you." They found a table in the cocktail lounge and ordered very dry martinis. A half hour later, a man wearing tasseled loafers and flannels and a navy-blue blazer with an insignia embroidered on the pocket came over and said, "Hello! My name's Freddy. And you're—?"

"Pearce," Eric said. "Mr. and Mrs. Pearce."

"Right!" said Freddy happily. "Just wanted to make sure." He went away, and they ordered another round of drinks. Everyone in the lounge seemed to know everyone else and everyone looked more or less drunk. Eric was beginning to feel drunk. "There aren't as many strangers here as there were last night," he said.

"Or we're stranger here than we were there," Sally said. "Or not as strange as they are here. Whatever."

"They're pretty strange," Eric said.

"They're wasp, though."

"Oh, they're one of us, all right," Eric said. "They're one of us."

Freddy summoned them to a table. "No slacks after six," he said when Sally stood up. He waggled a friendly finger at her. "But we'll let you in tonight."

The jacket of the pants suit was the length of a mini. Sally wore it for one in New York. "I'll take the pants off if it will make you feel better," she said sweetly to Freddy.

"Don't," Eric said. "You'll be cold."

They were given a table in a corner under pink fluorescent

lights. The waitress did not appear for a long time. They ordered rare filets and a bottle of St.-Émilion.

"A half bottle," the waitress said.

"A full bottle," Eric said.

"We're in the U.S.A., all right," said Sally.

They waited for their dinners and the wine, listening to the talk at the next table—two husbands and their wives.

"That's a great life they have down there in New York," one of the men was saying. "They turn in their wives the way I turn in cars." He had a buzz-saw voice. "You get tired of the wife after a few years, right? You meet some little blond number. You like her. So you divorce the wife and marry the blond. Nothing to it."

"What's wrong with that?" the other man said. "What's wrong with divorce if there aren't any kids? If two people don't get along? Where's the harm in that?"

One of the women was scandalized. "Do you realize what you're saying, George?" she cried. "You're saying that if there aren't any children there isn't any marriage!" She paused. "The vows don't count," she said, her voice rising. "The sacrament doesn't count. The *Church* doesn't count." She was almost screaming.

"Let's ask her what she thinks of premarital sexual relations," Sally said.

Strange music began drifting toward them from the cocktail lounge as they ate their dinner—noisy comic songs of the thirties and forties sung by Rudy Vallee and Spike Jones and Jimmy Durante, songs Eric remembered hearing on old 78's when he was a child. Eric and Sally stopped in the lounge on the way to their room. It was jammed. Under a spotlight at the far end stood a small man saying, "Ya better get back, lady, or I'll spit in ya face!" The crowd laughed. There was something odd about him; he seemed to be a hunchback or a dwarf, but from so far away it was hard for Eric to be sure. He wore a red paper derby and held a cigar, and he began to strut back and forth in the narrow space left clear for him, mouthing the words of a Durante song as a worn record played. "*Ink*-a-dink-a-*dink*. A-dink-a-*dink*. A-dink-a-DOO!" The audience kept egging him on. They were making fun of him.

"But he's a puppet," Sally said. "He's not human. It's the kind of thing I can't stand."

They turned to leave. Two fat women next to them smiled. "You should stay," one of them said. "You'll miss the best part of the show."

"God help him," Eric said when they were outside. "Do you think this goes on every Saturday night?"

The stars were brilliant; Orion floated over the trees. Towns like this were worse than the city, Eric thought. In New York you could escape the cruelty, perhaps, if you were lucky. In small towns the cruelty was focussed. No one was out of its range. He sometimes thought there might be no escape anywhere at all.

Back in their rooms, they changed into nightshirts and got into one of the beds. There was ice in the paper ice bucket still —Eric had left it outside the door—and they had vodkas on the rocks.

"I'm freaky," Sally said. "It was that guy, on top of everything else. That mechanical man. He was so *dead*. Mouthing those songs. . . ."

"The crowd was worse," Eric said.

"There was something wrong. I couldn't stand it. He was deformed."

"Drink," Eric said. They lit cigarettes.

"Neil was like that," Sally said, hunching her shoulders. Then she laughed, an odd hoot of a laugh. "I don't mean he was *deformed*," she said. "But he was mechanical, too. And I was going to *marry* him. Everything with him was always so planned. Even the spontaneous things were planned. I could so easily have married him. Not that I loved him, but he has money and he's sensible and we'd have had a ready-made circle of friends. Everything would have been all arranged. We'd be one of those modern New York couples."

"Don't look back," Eric said. "That's over."

"I know. I met you. I used to see Neil every day and I haven't seen him since the Wednesday after the Monday I met you. Was that cruel? He still calls me and tells me I'm cruel."

"You weren't cruel," Eric said. "Anything else drags out the pain. I know."

"Neil used to tell me, 'I'm going to make love to you every night and every morning so you'll never forget me.' He would wake me at six in the morning and make love to me before my body was awake, and at night I got so I turned my body off, too. I wasn't there with him but he didn't know that. So he couldn't touch me and I can forget him. I've forgotten him."

"We touch," Eric said.

"Oh, yes. We can really touch," Sally said. "We're the same species."

"What species?" Eric asked. They were touching now.

"Some kind of round furry beast. We're sensualists. Neil wasn't a sensualist. With him, it was all will. He *forced* everything, like that clown tonight."

"Touching is what really matters," Eric said.

"Yes. *C'est un question de peau.* That's Godard," Sally said. She broke off and looked at Eric. "What if we couldn't touch?" she said. "What if the day comes when we can't?"

It was what he had been thinking earlier, Eric thought. That, and that Sally might not love him. But she loved him, and they were touching now. "Don't look ahead, either," he said.

"It's funny," Sally said. "Sometimes I think of breaking off with you because I'm happy and I want to go back to Europe and be free, and I forget you're the reason I'm happy."

"We'll get back to Europe," Eric said, thinking of something else. "But there'll probably always be some pain. If you're in love, you open yourself to pain."

Sally sat up. "I didn't want to be in love with you," she said. "I really thought I'd wind up a cold bitch and now it looks like I'm not and it's not what I'd planned. Sometimes when I think how I love you I get a drowning feeling. But I'm happy."

"There's bound to be pain," Eric said. He had the feeling that he could see the course of his life grow clear before him. "You can't be open to pleasure the way we are and not be open to pain. If you won't take the pain, you're a rolling stone."

"I think I am a rolling stone," Sally said.

"You're not, not really," Eric said. "We're not. The thing is to stay open to it all."

But wouldn't that be impossible in the city? he thought. Already he had begun to close himself off, and it was only the beginning. What made him think he wouldn't wind up like the rest, with the New Haven Railroad and bridge and crosswords in the *Times?* "Let's get really drunk," he said.

"Be drunken!" Sally said. "*Enivrez-vous! Always be drunken, if you are not to be the martyred slave of Time!* That's Baudelaire. Of course, he didn't mean only booze."

But they were already drunken enough and now, suddenly, with a feeling of release, they turned to each other and made love quickly, exploding together, taken by surprise. As if their bodies were protesting these anxieties, this talk of pain.

Later Sally said to Eric, "You will always have to touch me a lot and make love to me a lot and abuse me. I don't mean *hurt* me. Turn me inside out. Make me feel things."

Eric said little more. All he could think of was how deep

they were going; it was mindless; it was beautiful; they made love with their bodies without giving it thought.

Screeching gulls woke them early in the morning and Eric went over to the window. "What do you know, we're on a pond!" he said. "It's frozen solid. The trees have ice on them and look like pink silver." Sally joined him. "They're like department-store trees," she said.

"I dreamed about you," she said to Eric while they were having breakfast in bed. "That's unusual, to have you in my dreams. You had a daughter. She had an apple in her hand. 'What will I do with this apple?' she said to you. 'I'm not sure I want it.' And you said, 'You will put it into your lunch bag and you will eat it.' "

"Would you like a free-form interpretation?" Eric said. "The daughter is you and the apple is love."

How happy they felt that morning! They left the inn late and drove north in bright sunshine through dune country that was wild and out of season. There was little snow and no ice. The swamp maples still held dry yellow leaves and the red maples glowed red. "We've been going in and out of winter since we started," Eric said. "Isn't it strange?"

They stopped at a Howard Johnson's in Hyannis for lunch, where local families were having their Sunday dinners and couples from out of town were eating their breakfast pancakes or eggs. "Ho-Jo's, the great leveler," Eric said. They had hamburgers, french fries, cole slaw, and milk.

A little afterward Eric pulled off the road and let Sally drive. She hadn't driven since she had come to New York; her license had expired. "Perhaps you'd better summarize the principles of driving for me as we go along," she said.

"How can you forget to drive? You can drive," Eric said.

But then there was the noise of a siren, growing louder, and a police car came straight toward them down the center of the road. Sally swerved abruptly onto the shoulder and stopped. The police car went past, an ambulance a hundred yards behind, its red light flashing. "I'm shaking," Sally said. "Please drive."

"Go ahead and drive," Eric said.

The sun was already low and they had been going to walk along a beach somewhere before the day was over. Near Wellfleet, Sally, who was driving comfortably now, turned off onto a smooth blacktop road that curved through dunes tufted with yellow grass and then went straight south paralleling a cliff. The sun was a bleached yellow and the horizon far off. The sea and sky were nearly the same color, the sea nearly calm. Sally parked and they got out of the car. The sound of the sea was as faint as on a day in summer. How warm the air was!

"It's the last day of the year," Eric said. "It's hard to believe."

The beach lay fifty feet below them and the way there was steep, down a sand cliff, though a dog's tracks ran up it. Far to the north three people were walking along the beach. A man in a hunting jacket and corduroys passed them striding southward and said, "Ayuh."

"There's so much *sky*," Sally said. "As much as in the desert." Eric took her picture against the yellow grass and the gray-green sea and sky, and she took his. "Smile," she said to him, holding the camera. "Don't smile. Frown. Look down. Look up. Look at me. Look away!"

"We could go down," Sally said. "But then we'd have to come back up."

"We can walk along the beach tomorrow," Eric said. "We have plenty of time for beaches."

They stood looking at the sea. "I didn't think I could drive any more, but you told me I could and I could," Sally said. "Just now I'm full of love for you."

They kissed. "We're both stars," Eric said.

"Whose movie?"

"Oh, Claude LeLouche, don't you think? *A Man and a Woman?* In the Camargue, with all these hazy yellows and blues and browns?"

"I'm happy," Sally said, holding Eric's hand. "Just now I'm really happy."

"I am too," Eric said.

"I can't see why we shouldn't stay happy," Sally said.

Eric drove the rest of the way into Provincetown, where they found a motel that looked out on salt marshes and dunes. It was nearly dark. They registered together, no longer uneasy about that, and the man at the desk took them to their room and turned on the lights and the TV set. Someone was interviewing four Americans in Stockholm. They were deserters from the Army.

"That one on the right looks like my brother," Sally said.

"Vietnam," Eric said. "I'd forgotten Vietnam."

He made Ricards. "Let's dress," Sally said. "It's New Year's Eve." They brought in the bags from the car. A thin rain had begun to fall.

The best place to eat was an inn nearby and they had wanted to walk there, but by the time they were ready the rain was heavy. Eric drove to the inn and dropped Sally at the door, then parked and ran back in the rain. Inside was another enormous restaurant; it was being remodelled and enlarged. "Can we have a drink in the bar before we eat?" Eric asked the hostess.

She laughed. "Oh, there's no bar," she said. "We're waiting for our liquor license. You bring your own."

Eric ran to the car and drove to the motel for the vodka. He came back and found Sally at a table by the windows that made up the restaurant's rear wall. Rain beat upon the panes and their backs were soon cold. Before them were what they were used to by now, family parties and parties of friends, some of them in evening dress tonight and some drinking champagne. There were so many of them—families much like the Pearces and the Rowlands. They appeared prosperous and stuffy and decorous and at their ease. "Where do they all come from?" Sally asked.

"They almost look happy tonight," Eric said.

"Families. Can you imagine having a family of your *own?*" Sally said. "We can't live like that."

"It doesn't have to be like that," Eric said. They both wanted to be attached, he thought—rooted somehow, and Sally as much as he, no matter what she might say. Yet how they both feared it! At this moment the people they saw looked almost all right, but then they were prettied up by the holiday glow. They were about as real as the characters in those old warm, human Hollywood movies of British life. When he and Sally looked at their parents' world what they saw was vulgar or shabby or corrupt or out-of-date or impure. Why should they attach themselves to the impure or the antique? But how could it ever be enough to be attached only to each other? Where were they to find their own kind?

They were tired by now of heavy meals, but they ordered the special dinner, lobster stuffed with crabmeat. After all, it was New Year's Eve and they were at the sea. They wished the vodka were champagne and drank it like champagne; the bottle was more than half empty by the time dinner was over. When they left, rain was still coming down hard and the wind was rising. Eric got the car and drove back for Sally, who stood waiting under the inn's flapping awning holding what was left of the vodka. They drove out to the tip of the Cape with some idea of drinking in the New Year at land's end, but there was nothing to see but rain and they were soon chilled through. They went back into Provincetown and found an open bar. It looked like an O'Neill set, Eric thought; fishnets, oars, and cork floats hung from walls and ceiling. Fishermen sat at the bar, and what looked like artists and students and their girls were at the tables. "I feel comfortable here," Sally said. "Me too," said Eric. The jukebox was playing the theme from "A Summer Place." The waitress wore a lowcut black dress and had a red-white-and-blue scarf tied above one knee like some lunatic decoration for gallantry in action. Eric and Sally took a table in the middle of the room and ordered beers. One of the men at the bar came over. "Happy New Year!" he said cheerfully. "Even to strangers."

"We may be strangers but we're friendly strangers," Eric said. "Happy New Year." But his speech was blurry and the man did not understand him. He went away. "But we're *friendly!*" Sally cried.

"I wish I were Irish," Eric said.

"It's all right in this place," Sally said. "We can stay."

They didn't stay long. The rain was still heavy and Eric kept taking the wrong turn and winding up at the municipal beach, but they were back in the motel before midnight even so, with Guy Lombardo on the TV screen and the sound turned low. They were very drunk. They pounced on each other. They went down on each other.

"I'm not one of your sweet suburban lovers," Eric said.

"Nail me, Eric," Sally cried. "Nail me. Nail me to the ground."

In the morning, Eric walked over to the inn for breakfast and let Sally sleep. The sky was blue and cloudless and the wind blew hard against him. It's blown the new year in, he thought. The dune grass was silver with rime, and thin ice coated the road. After he had finished breakfast, he ordered an o.j. and coffee to go for Sally and walked back to the motel with them, the wind now at his back. It was hard to stay on his feet. By the time he got to the motel, the coffee was cold.

He woke Sally and gave her an Alka-Seltzer. Then she drank

the orange juice and got out of bed. "It's winter now, all right," he said. He packed while Sally dressed, and went out to pay the man at the desk. "Quite a wind," the man said, and then he said, "Have a good year." He said it, Eric thought, the way people in New York said "Have a good day."

Eric was wearing fishnet long underwear and two sweaters under a parka. He gave Sally his down-filled vest to wear under her coat. They drove out to Race Point for a last look at the sea. "There were quite a few people having breakfast," Eric said to Sally in the car. "I missed you. I only ate half a stack of wheats."

"How many is that?"

"One and a half. Three halves, actually. I cut the stack down the middle. That's the first time we've been away from each other for nearly three days."

"What did you do without me?" Sally said.

"I looked out the window," Eric said. "The wind was snapping the awning and pieces of ice flew up and caught the sun like diamonds. And I listened to people talk. There was an old couple from Springfield at the next table, and just before they left another old couple from someplace on the Cape came over to say hello. It turned out they both knew a fellow in the insurance business from Boston named Jack Robinson—no kidding—and the Cape man said, 'Jack Robinson lost his wife last Sunday.'

" 'Lost his wife?' said the Springfield man, just as if he didn't know what the other fellow meant.

"The Cape man told him that the Robinsons had come up last week for the Christmas weekend and while they were out driving on Sunday she had a stroke and died right there in the car. And the Springfield man said, 'Why, that's terrible. Just terrible. I've known Jack for years. I've worked with him.' And do you know what his wife kept saying? All she could say was, over and over again, 'You'd think people would tell you. Imagine. This is the first time we've heard of it. You'd think people would let you know.' "

"They sound so bewildered," Sally said. "Let's not get old."

At Race Point, the roads leading to the parking area were icy and blocked by yellow sawhorses. Eric parked at the foot of the dunes and they walked across the sand up to the crest of the hill. Dry yellow beach grass grew out of the sand in a regular checkerboard pattern as if it had been seeded by machine. The grass was long and bent low under the wind. It was really cold. Dressed as warmly as they were, they were cold. The water was deep green, mottled white by choppy waves. The grass tossed and rippled like a horse's mane. How beautiful it all was! How free! "The wind is blowing through my head," Sally called to Eric over the wind's noise. "I could stay here for a long, long time just looking at the grass."

But it was too cold. Their ears began to hurt. They took each other's pictures there, then ran back to the car.

"Should we go into town and eat?" Eric said.

"No. Let's go right on."

"Good. The rain will be snow farther down."

"We missed our long walk on the beach."

"It doesn't matter. We'll come back when the winter is over," Eric said.

Soon Sally began to feel hungry, and Eric turned off at each exit looking for a place to eat. Already, there was more snow. Each side road led through a pretty Colonial town, quiet except for a few children sledding, and deposited them right back on the highway. There were no restaurants, no open stores.

The salt spreaders had been out early, and the highway was clear of snow but wet with salt water. Eric drove slowly, and the cars that passed them threw salt spray back on the windshield, speckling it until he could hardly see. He stopped at a gas station to have the windshield cleaned. A sign on the door read CLOSED JAN. 1. He took a canteen from the car and sloshed water on the windshield, then wiped it dry with a dirty shirt. Before the glass could dry the water had turned to a film of ice.

They went on past roads that led to beaches. "We could go down and look," Sally said.

"Food first," Eric said.

They finally found a restaurant open in Barnstable and had soup and hamburgers and milk there. Eric drank two glasses and Sally three. The attendant in the gas station next door cleaned the windshield again.

Soon after they left the Cape, the windshield began to cloud over once more. Traffic was heavier now. They were on a three-lane highway, the sun was nearer the horizon, and when they were going up a hill with the sun dead ahead Eric could not see the cars coming toward him through the glare. "It's weird," he said to Sally. "Half the time I can't see a thing."

"We could pull off and wait," Sally said. "In an hour the sun will be down."

"No," Eric said. "Let's go on. We're almost out of it. We'll be on the Interstate soon."

On the Interstate, with the median separating them from the oncoming traffic, driving seemed less hazardous at first. But now the sun was steadily in Eric's eyes. It must be in everyone's eyes, he thought. "This is wild," he said. "We're all driving straight into the sun and we're all blind."

"Can you see the car in front?" Sally asked.

"No. Can you?"

"No."

"But I know it's there," Eric said. He accelerated and a shape loomed before them. He slowed again. "Let's hope the guy behind didn't do that, too," he said. They went on.

"Isn't this risky?" Sally said after a few minutes.

"Sure," Eric said. "But I can't stop. It would be suicide to slow down. Does it feel dangerous?"

"Of course not," Sally said. "We're just sitting here, aren't we?" She giggled. "But I'm scared," she said.

"Don't worry. We lock in and trust to luck, that's all. It's the American way." He laughed, a little hysterically. "Mass man!" he said. "Lemmings! It's so symbolic. It turns me on. We're all driving like crazy and we're *blind!*"

But soon it was over. The sun dropped below the trees on the horizon and then below the horizon. They stopped for coffee at a place just off the highway, then went on. A few miles farther the traffic slowed, then stopped, then moved forward slowly, and they came to the scene of a multiple collision that must have happened only a few minutes before. A trailer truck had skidded and overturned and was jackknifed across two lanes, and fifteen or twenty cars were strewn beside the highway, some of them sunk to their hubcaps in snow on the median, some left cater-corner on the shoulders. Men and women and children stood wrapped in blankets like refugees at the side of the road. State police motioned the single line of traffic on by. Eric saw what looked like two bodies covered by blankets, but Sally was looking the other way and he said nothing. They passed a car whose windows had been smashed on one side. A blanket hung over the windows. There were people in the car; they could hear a dog or a baby whimpering.

Sally shivered. "It's so pointless," she said. "We could have been killed."

"It was pointless, all right," Eric said. He laughed, a sudden burst, and pulled Sally to him with his right arm. "We could have been killed," he said. "We could have been killed but we weren't. That's just the point. We *weren't*. Don't you see? It was really beautiful. All of us driving blind into the sun." Something had kept them safe, he thought. At that moment, he felt invincible. The fates were with them, he thought. They would survive. If only he hung on. If only he never lost his nerve.

By dark they were on the Connecticut Turnpike. Going this way the Cape wasn't nearly as far. At East Lyme they turned off and found a small restaurant a half mile down a snow-packed road. A fire burned in the fireplace. They ordered Scotches and drank them standing in front of the fire.

"We could make it into New York easily now," Eric said. "If you want."

"Let's wait until morning. Why hurl ourselves back?"

"There's the Rose Bowl game," Sally said. "We could stop and watch that."

They spent the night in Greenwich. Eric drove fast down the turnpike, going seventy-five to eighty and shifting lanes. "You're not driving like your father now," Sally said.

Snow was high in the town and their motel room was cold. They watched the last of the Rose Bowl game from bed under blankets, drinking the last of the Ricard. They ate, later, in a Chinese restaurant nearby, where they had beer and chicken chow mein and shrimp fried rice. Eric asked for chopsticks. They were heavy and bore the name of a Chinese restaurant in New Jersey. Balloons from a New Year's Eve party were scattered about on the floor. A waiter was picking them up and rubbing them against his sleeve, trying to get them to stick to the walls.

"I guess I'm sad," Sally said.

"It's the cold and having to go back," Eric said.

"I hate to say these end-of-the-trip things. But I sometimes have the feeling we're an ill-fated couple, that's all."

"We weren't ill-fated today," Eric said.

"I know. We were lucky. And it was a lovely trip. I had a good time."

"We're beating the odds," Eric said.

"Yes, perhaps we are."

"Where's the ill-fate, then?"

"I don't know. It's just a feeling. . . . If it's really as good as we think it is, how can it last?"

"If it's this good, why should it stop?"

"People change," Sally said. "They drift apart."

Not if they hang on, Eric thought. "Our bodies are the glue," he said.

"Already you're my second longest love," Sally said. "Neil was longer, but then I didn't love him. There was only my first love, in college, and in six months you'll be ahead."

"I'll wait," Eric said. "I'm serious. I want to marry you."

"Don't think about that."

"I'll wait," Eric said.

Sally said, "Take me home."

Their room was still cold. They made love under the blankets, and it was over in a few moments for them both. Everything was all right, Eric thought. They were still close. "We're like animals," Sally said before she could catch her breath. "Yes," Eric said. Their bodies were the glue. He could not believe that such happiness would not last.

The thermometer went down to zero during the night. They got up at seven and put on their city clothes in the bathroom with the hot shower running. They had no time for breakfast.

The sky was clear blue and there were fewer cars on the turnpike than they expected. For a while, approaching the turnpike, Eric had to drive into the sun, but after that it was behind him. "We never see the morning," Sally said. "It's so bright!"

By the time they reached the Bronx, traffic was heavy. Ahead of them across the East River rose the three great smoke-stacks of the Consolidated Edison plant; clouds of steam, bor-

dered with gold, stood above the stacks. Bridges, and trains
and cars on the bridges, crossed the river. Then there were more
stacks, more clouds of steam and smoke, more bridges, and over-
passes, and underpasses, and line upon line of cars. The sun's
brightness filled the air. Eric sat watching as he drove slowly
toward Manhattan and their jobs. The city, their enemy, had a
terrible beauty. "The city! It's like some fantastic dream," he
said. "My God, so much power!"

Sally was half asleep, her head upon his shoulder. "It's the
sun, not the city," she said. "The power is in the sun."

She was right, of course, Eric thought, but how easy it was
to forget it. How quickly the city took you in.

They drove over the Triborough Bridge and then down
Park Avenue until they came to the rows of glass buildings that
reflect each other and the sky. Eric stopped in front of the building where Sally worked. He kissed her. *"Ciao,"* he said. He was
casual now. "Have dinner with me tonight."

"Ciao," Sally said lightly. She, too, was speaking as if nothing had changed or would ever change. "Let's go to the Greek
place," she said, "and drink *ouzo* there."

They were married in Wilmington, in the Cathedral Church
of St. John, that fall. It was a beautiful wedding. Most of the
Pearces, from Indiana and Ohio and Kentucky, were there, and
all of the Rowlands, even Grandpa Rowland, quiet and very
much his old self, who had been brought down from the hospital for the day.

The Girl Who Sang with the Beatles

Of course their tastes turned out to be different. Cynthia was twenty-eight when they married, and looked younger, in the way small, very pretty women can—so much younger sometimes that bartenders would ask for her I.D. Larry was close to forty and gray, a heavy man who, when he moved, moved slowly. He had been an English instructor once, though now he wrote market-research reports, and there was still something bookish about him. Cynthia, who was working as an interviewer for Larry's company when he met her, had been a vocalist with several dance bands for a while in the fifties before she quit to marry her first husband. She had left high school when she was a junior to take her first singing job. She and Larry were from different generations, practically, and from different cultures, and yet when they were married they both liked the same things. That was what brought them together. Thirties movies. Old bars—not the instant-tradition places but what was left of the old ones, what Cynthia called the bar bars. Double features in the loge of the Orpheum, eating hot dogs and drinking smuggled beer. Gibsons before dinner and Scotch after. Their TV nights, eating delicatessen while they watched "Mr. Lucky" or "Route 66" or "Ben Casey," laughing at the same places, choking up at the same places, howling together when something was just too *much*. And then the eleven-o'clock news and the Late and Late Late Shows, while they drank and necked and sometimes made love. And listening to Cynthia's records—old Sinatras and Judys, and Steve and Eydie, or "The Fantasticks" or "Candide." They even agreed on redecorating Cynthia's apartment, which was full of leftovers from her first marriage. They agreed on all of it—the worn (but genuine) Oriental rugs; the low carved Spanish tables; the dusky colors, grays and mauve and rose; the damask sofa with its down pillows; and, in the bedroom, the twin beds, nearly joined but held separate by an ornate brass bedstead. Cynthia's old double bed had been impractical; Larry was too big, and Cynthia kicked. When they came back from their Nassau honeymoon and saw the apartment for the first time in ten days, Cynthia said, "God, Larry, I *love* it. It's pure *Sunset Boulevard* now."

The place made Larry think of Hyde Park Boulevard in Chicago, where he had grown up in a mock-Tudor house filled with the wrought iron and walnut of an earlier Spanish fad. Entering the apartment was like entering his childhood. "Valencia!" sang in his head. "Valencia! In my dreams it always seems I hear you softly call to me. Valencia!"

They were married in the summer of 1962 and by the spring of 1963 the things they had bought no longer looked quite right. Everyone was buying Spanish now, and there was too much around in the cheap stores. Larry and Cynthia found themselves in a dowdy apartment full of things that looked as if they had been there since the twenties. It was depressing. They began to ask each other what they had done. Not that either of them wanted out, exactly, but what had they done? Why had they married? Why couldn't they have gone on with their affair? Neither had married the other for money, that was certain. Larry had made Cynthia quit work (not that she minded) and now they had only his salary, which was barely enough.

"We still love each other, don't we? I mean, I know I love

you." Cynthia was in Larry's bed and Larry was talking. It was three in the morning, and they had come back from their usual Saturday-night tour of the neighborhood bars. "I love you," Larry said.

"You don't like me."

"I *love* you, Cynthia."

"You don't like me." Propped up by pillows, she stared red-eyed at a great paper daisy on the wall.

"I love you, Cindy."

"So? Big deal. Men have been telling me they loved me since I was fourteen. I thought you were different."

Larry lay flat on his back. "Don't be tough. It's not like you," he said.

"I *am* tough. That's what you won't understand. You didn't marry *me*. You married some nutty idea of your own. I was your secret fantasy. You told me so." Cynthia was shivering.

"Lie down," Larry said. "I'll rub your back."

"You won't get around me that way," Cynthia said, lying down. "You tricked me. I thought you liked the things I liked. You won't even watch TV with me anymore."

Larry began to rub the back of Cynthia's neck and play with the soft hairs behind one ear.

"Why don't you ever watch with me?" Cynthia said.

"You know. I get impatient."

"You don't like me." Cynthia was teasing him by now. "If you really liked me, you'd watch," she said. "You'd *like* being bored."

Larry sat up. "That isn't it," he said. "You know what it is? It's the noise. All the things you like make *noise*."

"I read."

"Sure. With the radio or the stereo or the TV on. I can't. I have to do one thing at a time," Larry said. "What if I want to sit home at night and read a book?"

"So read."

"When you have these programs you quote have to watch unquote?"

"Get me headphones. That's what my first husband did when he stopped talking to me. Or go in the bedroom and shut the door. I don't mind."

"We'll do something," Larry said, lying down again. "Now let's make love."

"Oh, it's no use, Larry," Cynthia said. "Not when we're like this. I'll only sweat."

And so it went on many nights, and everything seemed tainted by their disagreements, especially their times in bed. After they had made love, they would slip again into these exchanges, on and on. What Cynthia seemed to resent most was that Larry had not been straightforward with her. Why had he let her think he cared for her world of song and dance? She knew it was trivial. She had never tried to make him think she was deep. Why had he pretended he was something he wasn't?

How was Larry to tell her the truth without making her think he was either a snob or a fool? There was no way. The thing was, he said, that when they met he *did* like what she liked, period. Just because she liked it. What was wrong with that? He wanted to see her enjoying herself, so they did what she wanted to do—went to Radio City to see the new Doris Day, or to Basin Street East to hear Peggy Lee, or to revivals of those fifties musicals Cynthia liked so much. Forget the things he liked if she didn't—foreign movies and chamber music and walks in Central Park, all that. She must have known what he liked, after all. She had been in his apartment often enough before they were married, God knows. She had seen his books and records. She knew his tastes.

"I thought you gave all that up," Cynthia said. "I thought you'd changed."

"I thought you *would* change," Larry said. "I thought you

wanted to. I thought if you wanted to marry me you must want to change."

"Be an *intellectual?*" Cynthia said. "You must be kidding."

No, he was serious. Why didn't she get bored with the stuff she watched and the junk she read? *He* did. When you had seen three Perry Masons, you had seen them all, and that went for Doris Day movies, the eleven-o'clock news, and "What's My Line?"

"I know all that," Cynthia said. She *liked* to be bored. God, you couldn't keep thinking about *reality* all the time. You'd go out of your mind. She liked stories and actors that she knew, liked movies she had seen a dozen times and books she could read over and over again. Larry took his reading so seriously. As if reading were *life*.

Larry tried to persuade himself that Cynthia was teasing him, but it was no use. She meant what she said. She *liked East of Eden, Marjorie Morningstar, Gone with the Wind*. She liked Elizabeth Taylor movies. She found nourishment in that Styrofoam. He could see it in her childlike face, which sometimes shone as if she were regarding the beatific vision when she was under the spell of the sorriest trash. What repelled him brought her to life. He could feel it in her when they touched and when, after seeing one of her favorite movies, they made love. How odd that he should have married her! And yet he loved her, he thought, and he thought she loved him—needed him, anyway.

Sometimes they talked of having a child, or of Cynthia's going back to work or of attending night classes together at Columbia or the New School, but nothing came of it. They were both drinking too much, perhaps, and getting too little exercise, yet it was easier to let things go on as they were. Larry did set out to read Camus, the first serious reading he had done since their marriage, and in the evenings after dinner he would go into the bedroom, shut the door, turn on WNCN to muffle the sounds from the living room, put Flents in his ears, and read. Although the meaningless noises from the TV set—the not quite comprehensible voices, the sudden surges of music—still reached him, he was reluctant to buy Cynthia the headphones she had suggested. They would be too clear a symbol of their defeat.

Cynthia often stayed up until three or four watching the late movies or playing her records, and Larry, who usually fell asleep around midnight, would sometimes wake after two or three hours and come out of the bedroom shouting "Do you know what *time* it is?" and frighten her. Sometimes, though, he would make a drink for himself and watch her movie, too, necking with her the way they used to do, without saying much. They were still drawn to each other.

Sometimes, very late at night when she was quite drunk, Cynthia would stand before the full-length mirror in their bedroom and admire herself. "I'm beautiful," she would say. "Right now, I'm really beautiful, and who can see me?" Larry would watch her from the bed. Something slack in her would grow taut as she looked in the mirror. She would draw her underpants down low on her hips, then place her hands on her shoulders, her crossed arms covering her bare breasts, and smile at her reflection, a one-sided smile. "I'm a narcissist," she would say, looking at Larry in the mirror. "I'm a sexual narcissist. How can you stand me?" Then she would join Larry in his bed.

Larry couldn't deny Cynthia anything for long. If he insisted on it, she would turn off the set, but then she would sulk until he felt he had imposed upon her, and he would turn the set back on or take her out for a drink. How could he blame her? They had so little money. What else was there for her to do?

One Saturday night after their tour of the bars, Cynthia changed clothes and came out of the bedroom wearing a twenties black dress and black net stockings and pumps. The dress was banded with several rows of fringe and stopped just at the knee.

She had had to add the last row of fringe, she told Larry. Her first husband had made her, just before they went to a costume party, because the dress showed too much of her thighs. Larry knelt before her and tore off the last row. Cynthia danced for him (a Charleston, a shimmy, a Watusi) and after that she sang. She had sung to him now and then late at night before they were married—just a few bars in a soft, almost inaudible voice. Tonight the voice seemed full and touching to Larry, and with a timbre and sadness different from any voice he had ever heard. "*Like* me. Please like me," the voice seemed to say. "Just like me. That's all I need. I'll be nice then." She might have been the star she wanted to be, Larry thought. She had the charm and the need for love, but perhaps the voice was too small and her need too great. She had told him that twice while she was singing with a band in Las Vegas she had been "discovered" by assistant directors and offered a movie audition, and that each time she had been sick in the studio—literally sick to her stomach—and unable to go on. She had been too scared. Yet she still might have a career somehow, Larry thought. He could encourage her to practice. It would be an interest for her—something to do. She was barely past thirty and looked less. There was time.

Larry decided to read Camus in French and to translate some of the untranslated essays, just for practice, into English. One night he came home with the headphones Cynthia wanted, the old-fashioned kind made of black Bakelite, and hooked them up to the TV set through a control box that had an off-on switch for the speaker. Now that he could blank out the commercials, Larry would watch with Cynthia now and then— some of the news specials, and the Wide World of Sports, and the late-night reruns of President Kennedy's press conferences, one of the few things they both enjoyed. They could both acknowledge his power, pulsing in him and out toward them—that sure, quick intelligence and that charm.

Cynthia was happier now, because with the headphones on and the speakers off she could watch as late as she wanted without being afraid of Larry. When the phone rang, she would not hear it. Larry would answer, finally, and if it was for her he would stand in front of the set gesturing until she took the headphones off. She would sit on the sofa for hours, dressed as if for company, her eyes made up to look even larger than they were, wearing one of the at-home hostessy things from Jax or Robert Leader she had bought before they were married, which hardly anyone but she and Larry had ever seen. Looking so pretty, and with those radio operator's black headphones on her ears.

The sight made Larry melancholy, and he continued to work lying on his bed, propped up with a writing board on his lap. He would hear Cynthia laughing sometimes in the silent living room, and now and then, hearing thin sounds from her headphones, he would come out to find her crying, the phones on her lap and the final credits of a movie on the screen. "I always cry at this one," she would say. With the headphones, Cynthia was spending more time before the set than ever. Larry encouraged her to sing—to take lessons again if she wanted. But she did sing, she said, in the afternoons. She sang with her records, usually. There were a few songs of Eydie's and Peggy's and Judy's she liked. She sang along with those.

In spite of everything, when Larry compared his life now with his first marriage or with the bitter years after that, he could not say that this was worse. Cynthia seemed almost content. She made no demands upon him and left him free to think or read what he pleased. But there were nights when he would put his book aside and lie on his bed, hearing Cynthia laugh now and then or get up to make herself another drink, and ask himself why he was there. Little, in his job or in his life, seemed reasonable or real.

Why had he fallen in love with Cynthia? It was just because she was so *American*, he decided one night. She *liked* canned chili and corned-beef hash, the Academy Awards, cole slaw, barbecued chicken, the Miss America contest, head lettuce with Russian dressing, astrology columns, *Modern Screen*, takeout pizza pies. She liked them and made faces at them at the same time, looking up or over at him and saying, "Oh God, isn't this awful? Isn't this vile?" Everything he had turned his back on in the name of the Bauhaus and the Institute of Design, of Elizabeth David and James Beard, of Lewis Mumford, Paul Goodman, D. H. Lawrence, Henry Miller, Frank Lloyd Wright—here it all was dished up before him in Cynthia. All the things that (to tell the truth) he had never had enough of. He had lost out on them in high school, when he had really wanted them, because he was studious and shy. He had rejected them in college, where it was a matter of political principle among his friends to reject them, before he had the chance to find out what they were like. At thirty-eight, when he met Cynthia, what did he know? Weren't there vast areas of the American experience that he had missed? Why, until Cynthia he had never shacked up in a motel. Nor had he ever been in a barroom fight, or smoked pot, or been ticketed for speeding, or blacked out from booze.

What had he fallen in love with, then, but pop America! One more intellectual seduced by kitsch! He could almost see the humor in it. It was the first solid discovery about himself he had made for years, and he lay back in his bed, smiling. How glittering Cynthia's world had seemed, he thought. The sixties —this is what they *were!* Thruways, motels, Point Pleasant on a Saturday night twisting to the juke! That trip to Atlantic City in winter where, at the Club Hialeah, the girls from South Jer-

sey danced on the bar, and in the Hotel Marlborough-Blen-
heim he and Cynthia wandered through the cold deserted cor-
ridors and public rooms like actors in a shabby *Marienbad*. And
the music! Miles, Monk, Chico, Mingus, the M.J.Q., Sinatra
and Nelson Riddle, Belafonte, Elvis, Ray Charles, Dion, Lena
Horne—all new to him. He had stopped listening to music before bop, and with Cynthia he listened to everything. Progressive
or pop or rhythm and blues, whatever. Did he like it all—how
was it possible to like it *all?*—because Cynthia did, or did he
fall in love with Cynthia because she liked it all? What difference
did it make? It was all new—a gorgeous blur of enthusiasms.
For the first time in his life he had given himself away. How
wonderful it had been, at thirty-eight, on the edge of middle
age—*in* middle age—to play the fool! This was experience, this
was *life*, this was the sixties—*his* generation, with his peers in
charge, the Kennedys and the rest. Wasn't that coming alive,
when you were free enough to play the fool and not care? And
if there had been enough money, he and Cynthia might have
kept it up. . . . They might.

Yet hardly a moment had passed during the first months
with Cynthia when he did not know what he was doing. He
had got into a discussion of pop culture one night in the Cedar
Street Tavern not long after he and Cynthia were married.
"You don't know what you're talking about," he had said to
the others while Cynthia was on a trip to the head. "You only
dip into it. Listen. You don't know. I've *married* it. I've married the whole great American *schmier*."

But how nearly he had been taken in! Cynthia never had.
She knew show business from the inside, after all. She dug it,
and liked it, and laughed at herself for liking it. She knew how
shabby it was. Yet it did something for her—that trumpery,
that fake emotion, that sincere corn. Once he found out something was bad, how could he care for it any longer? It was
impossible. If he had gone overboard at first for Cynthia's world,

wasn't that because it was new to him and he saw fresh energy there? And how spurious that energy had turned out to be—how slick, how manufactured, how dead! And how dull. Yet something in it rubbed off on Cynthia, mesmerized her, and made her glamorous, made her attractive to him still. That was the trouble. He still wanted her. He was as mesmerized as she. Wasn't it the fakery he despised that shone in Cynthia and drew him to her? Then what in their marriage was real? He felt as detached from his life as a dreamer at times feels detached from his dream.

Quiet and sedentary as it had become, Larry's life continued to be charged with a forced excitement. The pop love songs, the photographs of beautiful men and women in the magazines Cynthia read, the romantic movies on TV, Cynthia herself—changing her clothes three or four times a day as if she were the star in a play and Larry the audience—all stimulated him in what he considered an unnatural way. He recognized in himself an extravagant lust that was quickly expended but never spent when he and Cynthia made love, as if she were one of the idealized photographs of which she was so fond and he were returning within her to the fantasies of his adolescence, their intercourse no more than the solitary motions of two bodies accidentally joined.

"We shouldn't have got married," Cynthia said one hot Saturday night in the summer of 1963 as they were lying in their beds trying to fall asleep.

"Maybe not," Larry said.

"Marriage turns me off. Something happens. I told you."

"I didn't believe you," Larry said. "And anyway we're married."

"We sure are."

"I picked a lemon in the garden of love," Larry said. Cynthia laughed and moved into Larry's bed.

Late that night, though, he said something else. "We're like

Catholics and their sacrament," he said. "When you're married for the second time, you're practically stuck with each other. You've almost got to work it out."

"You may think you're stuck, but *I'm* not," Cynthia said, and moved back to her own bed. The next Saturday night she brought up what Larry had said about being "stuck." Why had he said it? Didn't he know her at all? Whenever she felt bound she had to break free—right out the door, sooner or later. That was what had always happened. Was he trying to drive her away? He knew how independent she'd been. That's what he liked about her, he'd said once. All that talk about protecting each other's freedom! What a lot of crap. Look at them now. Two birds in a cage, a filthy cage.

Cynthia's anger frightened Larry, and, to his surprise, the thought of her leaving frightened him, too. But nothing changed. There wasn't much chance of her breaking away, after all. They didn't have enough money to separate, and neither of them really wanted to—not *that* routine, not again.

More and more often now Larry would sit in the living room reading while Cynthia watched her programs, headphones on her ears. He would look over at her, knowing that at that moment she was content, and feel some satisfaction, even a sense of domestic peace. At times he would lie with his head on Cynthia's lap while she watched, and she would stroke his hair.

One payday Larry came home with a second pair of headphones, made of green plastic and padded with foam rubber, the sort disc jockeys and astronauts wear, and plugged them into the stereo through a box that permitted turning off the speakers. Now he, like Cynthia, could listen in silence. He stacked some of his records on the turntable—the Mozart horn concertos, a Bach cantata, Gluck. It was eerie, Larry thought, for them both to be so completely absorbed, sitting twenty feet apart in that silent living room, and on the first night he found himself watching Cynthia's picture on the TV screen as **the** music in his ears seemed to fade away. Finally, he took off his earphones, joined Cynthia on the sofa, and asked her to turn on the sound. After a few nights, however, the sense of eeriness wore off, and Larry was as caught up in his music as Cynthia was in her shows. The stereo sound was so rich and pure; unmixed with other noises, the music carried directly into his brain, surrounding and penetrating him. It was so intense, so mindless. Listening was not a strong enough word for what was happening. The music flowed through him and swallowed him up. He felt endowed with a superior sense, as if he were a god. Yet there was something illicit about their both finding so intense a pleasure in isolation. He was troubled, off and on, by what they were falling into, but their life was tranquil and that was almost enough.

One night when Larry was reading (something he rarely did now) and there was nothing on TV she cared for, Cynthia put some of her records on the turntable and Larry's headphones on her ears and listened to Eydie and Judy and Frank, dancing a few steps now and then and singing the words softly. "Why didn't you tell me!" she said. It was *fantastic*. She could hear all the bass, and the color of the voices, and things in some of the arrangements she had never known were there. More and more often as the summer wore on, Cynthia would listen to her music instead of watching the tube, and Larry, thinking this a step in the right direction—toward her singing, perhaps— turned the stereo over to her several evenings a week and tried to concentrate again on his reading. But music now held him in a way books no longer could, and after a few weeks he bought a second stereo phonograph and a second set of headphones. By the fall of 1963, he and Cynthia had begun to listen, each to his own music, together. "This is really a kick," Cynthia would say. The intensity of it excited them both.

On the day President Kennedy was assassinated, Larry and Cynthia were having one of their rare lunches in midtown at an Italian place near Bloomingdale's, where Cynthia planned to go shopping afterward. There was a small television set above the restaurant bar, and people stood there waiting for definite news after the first word of the shooting. When it was clear that the President was dead, Larry and Cynthia went back to their apartment. Larry didn't go back to work. They watched television together that afternoon and evening, and then they went to bed and began to weep. When Larry stopped, Cynthia would sob, and then Larry would start again. So it went until after four in the morning, when they fell asleep. Until the funeral was over, Cynthia sat before the set most of the day and night. Much of the time she was crying, and every night when she came to bed the tears would start. Larry, dry-eyed sooner than she was, was at first sympathetic, then impatient, then annoyed.

"He was such a *good* man," Cynthia would say, or "He was *ours*. He was all we had," and after the burial she said, half smiling, "He was a wonderful star." Nothing in her actual life could ever move her so deeply, Larry thought. How strange, to feel real sorrow and weep real tears for an unreal loss! But she was suffering, no question of that, and she could not stop crying. The Christmas season came and went, and she still wept. She had begun to drink heavily, and often Larry would put her to bed. On the edge of unconsciousness, she would continue to cry.

What was she, he thought, but a transmitter of electronic sensations? First she had conveyed the nation's erotic fantasies to him, and now it was the national sorrow, and one was as unreal as the other. But there was more to it than that. John Kennedy had been a figure in her own erotic fantasies. She had told Larry so. She wept for him as a woman would for her dead lover. She was like a woman betrayed by Death, Larry thought, when what had betrayed her was the television set she had counted upon to shield her from the real. It had always told her stories of terror and passion that, because they were fictitious, might be endured, and now it had shown her actual death and actual sorrow. There was no way to console her, because her loss was not an actual loss, and Larry began to think her suffering more than he could endure. He began to wonder if she might not have lost her mind.

Cynthia read nothing for weeks after the assassination but articles on it, and so she did not hear of the Beatles until Larry, hoping to distract her, brought home their first album. She thought little of it at first, but after the Beatles appeared on the Ed Sullivan Show in February she became an admirer and then a devotee. Larry brought her the new Beatles 45's as they came out, and he stood in line with teen-age girls at the newsstands on Forty-second Street to buy the Beatles fan magazines. "I guess the period of mourning is over," Cynthia said one Saturday night. She still saved articles about the assassination, though, and photographs of Jacqueline in black.

When Cynthia began to sing as she listened to the Beatles late at night, Larry, listening from the bedroom, was pleased. She would play their records over and over, accompanying them in a voice that seemed flat and unresonant, perhaps because with the headphones on she could not hear the sounds she made. She no longer wept, or Larry was asleep when she did.

One night, Larry woke around three to the tinny noise of "I Want to Hold Your Hand" spilling from Cynthia's phones and found he was hungry. On his way to the kitchen, he stopped in the dark hall to watch Cynthia, who stood in the center of the living room with the astronaut headphones on, singing what sounded like a harmonizing part, a little off-key, holding an imaginary guitar, swaying jerkily, and smiling as if she were before an audience. Her performance, empty as it was, seemed oddly polished and professional. Afraid of startling her, he stood watching until the end of the song before he entered the room.

"How much did you see?" Cynthia said.

"Nothing," Larry said. "I was going to get a glass of milk, that's all." The look on Cynthia's face as she stood before him with those enormous headphones clamped to her ears troubled him, as if he had discovered her in some indeceny better forgotten. "After this I'll flick out the lights and warn you," he said.

And he said no more about it, though often now he awoke during the night to the faint sounds from Cynthia's headphones and wondered what she was doing that held her so fast. He was jealous of it in a way. She was rarely in bed before four, and always in bed when he left for work in the morning. In the evening, though, as she watched television, she seemed happy enough, and much as she had been before Kennedy's death.

For some time after the assassination, they gave up their Saturday nights in the bars, but by April they were again making their rounds. Once, when they came home higher and happier than usual, Cynthia danced and sang for Larry as she had before, and for a while Larry danced with her, something he did not do often. They were having such a pleasant time that when Larry put on a Beatles album and Cynthia began her performance for him, she explained. "We're at the Palladium in London, you see," she said. "The place is mobbed. . . . The Beatles are onstage. . . . I'm singing with them, and naturally everybody loves us. I work through the whole show . . . playing second guitar. I back up George." And then she sang, a third or so below the melody, " 'She was just seventeen if you know what I mean. . . .' "

"I never sing lead," Cynthia said when the number was over. "I play a minor rôle."

"Is this what you do at night?" Larry asked her.

Cynthia was breathing heavily. "Sure," she said. "It sounds

silly, but it's not. Besides, it's possible, isn't it? It *could* happen. I can sing." She looked at Larry, her eyes candid and kind. "Don't worry," she said. "I'm not losing my grip."

"It's a nice game," Larry said later when they were in bed.

"Oh, it's more than a game," Cynthia said. "When I'm with them in the Palladium, I'm really *there*. It's more real than here. I know it's a fantasy, though."

"How did you meet the Beatles?" Larry asked her.

"D'you really want to hear?" Cynthia said. She seemed pleased at his interest, Larry thought, but then she was drunk. They both were.

"It's not much of a story," she said. "The details vary, but basically I am standing on Fifth Avenue there near the Plaza in the snow waiting for a cab at three in the afternoon, dressed in my black flared coat and black pants and the black boots you gave me, and I have a guitar. No taxis, or they're whipping right by, and I'm *cold*. You know how cold I can get. And then this Bentley stops with a couple of guys in front and in back is George Harrison all alone, though sometimes it's Paul. He gives me a lift and we talk. He's completely polite and sincere, and I can see he likes me. It seems the Beatles are rehearsing for a television special at Central Plaza and they'll be there the next day, so he asks me to come up and bring my guitar. I go, naturally, and it turns out they are auditioning girls, and I'm the winner. What would be the point if I wasn't? They want a girl for just one number, but when they see how terrific I am, of course they love me, and when they find out I've already worked up all their songs I'm in."

"You join them."

"Sure. They insist. I have to leave you, but you don't mind, not anymore. In one year, we're The Beatles and Cynthia and we're playing the Palladium, and Princess Margaret and Tony are there, and Frank, and Peter O'Toole, and David McCallum, and Steve McQueen, and Bobby Kennedy. And all those men *want* me, I can feel it, and I'm going to meet them afterward at the Savoy in our suite."

" 'Our'?"

"I'm married to a rich diamond merchant who lets me do whatever I want. Played by George Sanders."

"I thought you were married to me," Larry said.

"Oh, no. You divorced me, alleging I was mentally cruel. Maybe I was once, but I'm not anymore, because the Beatles love me. They're my brothers. They're not jealous of me at all."

"Are you putting me on?" Larry said.

"No. Why should I? I made it all up, if that's what you mean, but I *really* made it up."

"Do you believe any of it?" Larry said.

Cynthia smiled at him. "Don't you? You used to say I had a good voice and you used to say I was pretty. Anyway, I don't have fantasies about things that couldn't possibly happen. I could get a job tomorrow if you'd let me."

Cynthia's voice had the lilt Larry remembered from the days before they were married. The whole thing was so convincing and so insane. He began to indulge her in it. "I'm going to Beatle now," Cynthia would say nearly every night after dinner, and Larry would go into the bedroom. Whenever he came out, he would flick the hall lights and she would stop. She was shy and did not let him watch often at first. She seemed embarrassed that she had told him as much as she had—if, indeed, she remembered telling him anything at all.

Larry liked the Beatles more and more as the nights went by, and often he would listen to their records with the speakers on before Cynthia began her performance. "Listen, Cynthia," he said one Saturday night. "The Beatles are filled with the Holy Ghost." He was really quite drunk. "Do you know that? They came to bring us back to life! Out of the old nightmare. Dallas, Oswald, Ruby, all of it, cops, reporters, thruways, lies, crises, missiles, heroes, cameras, fear—all that mishmash, and all of it dead. All of us dead watching the burial of the dead. Look at *you*. They've brought you back to life. I couldn't—not after November. Nothing could."

"You're right," Cynthia said. "I didn't want to tell you. I thought you'd be jealous."

"Jealous? Of the Beatles?"

"They're very real to me, you know."

"I'm not jealous," Larry said.

"Then will you read to me the way you used to? Read me to sleep?"

"Sure."

"Can I get in your bed?"

"Sure."

Before Larry had finished a page, he was asleep, and Cynthia was asleep before him.

For her birthday in September, Larry gave Cynthia an electric guitar. Though she could not really play it and rarely even plugged it in, she used the guitar now in her performances, pretending to pluck the strings. She began to dress more elaborately for her Beatling, too, making up as if for the stage.

She was a little mad, no question of it, Larry thought, but it did no harm. He no longer loved her, nor could he find much to like in her, and yet he cared for her, he felt, and he saw that she was too fragile to be left alone. She was prettier now than he had ever seen her. She *should* have been a performer. She needed applause and admirers and whatever it was she gave herself in her fantasies—something he alone could not provide. Their life together asked little of him at any rate, and cost little. By now he and Cynthia rarely touched or embraced; they were like old friends—fellow-conspirators even, for who knew of Cynthia's Beatle world but him?

Cynthia discussed her performances with Larry now, telling

him of the additions to her repertoire and of the new places she and the Beatles played—Kezar Stadium, the Hollywood Bowl, Philharmonic Hall. She began to permit him in the living room with her, and he would lie on the sofa listening to his music while her Beatling went on. He felt sometimes that by sharing her fantasies he might be sharing her madness, but it seemed better for them both to be innocently deranged than to be as separate as they had been before. All of it tired Larry, though. He was past forty. He felt himself growing old, and his tastes changing. Now he listened to the things he had liked in college —the familiar Beethoven and Mozart symphonies, and Schubert, and Brahms, in new stereophonic recordings. Often as he listened he would fall asleep and be awakened by the silence when the last of the records stacked on the turntable had been played. Usually Cynthia's performance would still be going on, and he would rise, take off his headphones and go to bed.

One night Larry fell asleep toward the end of the "Messiah," with the bass singing "The trumpet shall sound . . ." and the trumpet responding, and woke as usual in silence, the headphones still on his ears. This time, he lay on the sofa looking at Cynthia, his eyes barely open. She had changed clothes again, he saw, and was wearing the silver lamé pants suit, left over from her singing days, that she had worn the first night he had come to her apartment. He saw her bow, prettily and lightly in spite of the headphones on her ears, and extend her arms to her imaginary audience. Then he watched her begin a slow, confined dance, moving no more than a step to the side or forward and then back. She seemed to be singing, but with his headphones on Larry could not hear. She raised her arms again, this time in a gesture of invitation, and although she could not know he was awake it seemed to Larry that she was beckoning to him and not to an imaginary partner—that this dance, one he had never seen, was for him, and Cynthia was asking him to join her in that slow and self-contained step.

Larry rose and sat looking at her, his head by now nearly clear. "Come," she beckoned. "Come." He saw her lips form the word. Was it he to whom she spoke or one of her fantasies? What did it matter? She stood waiting for her partner—for him— and Larry got up, unplugged his headphones, and walked across the room to her. The movement seemed to him a movement of love. He plugged his headphones in next to Cynthia's and stood before her, almost smiling. She smiled, and then, in silence, not quite touching her in that silent room, with the sound of the Beatles loud in his ears, Larry entered into her dance.

A NOTE ON THE TYPE

This book was set on the Linotype in Fairfield, the first type face from the hand of the distinguished American artist and engraver Rudolph Ruzicka. In its structure Fairfield displays the sober and sane qualities of a master craftsman whose talent has long been dedicated to clarity. It is this trait that accounts for the trim grace and virility, the spirited design and sensitive balance of this original type face.

Rudolph Ruzicka was born in Bohemia in 1883 and came to America in 1894. He set up his own shop devoted to wood engraving and printing in New York in 1913, after a varied career as wood engraver, in photoengraving and bank-note printing plants, and as art-director and free-lance artist. He has designed and illustrated many books and has created a considerable list of individual prints—wood engravings, line engravings on copper, aquatints.

Composed, printed, and bound by The Colonial Press Inc., Clinton, Massachusetts.